BRAND OF A TEXAN

The rider on the gelding stared down at the frontier town. It had changed a great deal since he saw it last—but then so had he. His memories of the place were bitter ones because it was here, more than five years ago, that a mob had beaten him for his Union sympathies and then driven him out.

Well, now Ruel Crockett was coming back. He hunched his wide shoulders slightly and urged the gelding forward with his knees, holding the bridle in his left hand—which meant his right hand was free, ready to drop down to his trusty Colt.

BRAND OF A TEXAN

Steven C. Lawrence

GUNSMOKE

First published in the UK by Chivers

This hardback edition 2005
by BBC Audiobooks Ltd
by arrangement with
Golden West Literary Agency

ISBN 1 4056 8024 5

British Library Cataloguing in Publication Data available.

Printed and bound in Great Britain by
Antony Rowe Ltd., Chippenham, Wiltshire

Chapter One

TIME had made changes in Hobart, just as it had worked its changes in the rider who pulled up for a smoke at the edge of the moss-hung oak grove a quarter-mile north of the frontier town. In the blistering noonday Texas sun the shade offered no coolness, only less heat. Ruel Crockett's face was thoughtful, the cigarette between his fingers forgotten as he spoke to the claybank gelding cropping at the grama grass.

"Not long now, King," he said. "You'll have your own stall tonight."

When he'd first seen the town after topping a long sloping rise of prairie, the growth of Hobart had surprised him. New false-fronted buildings rose along Pioneer Street, three of them two-story structures that crowded out the smaller buildings—the picket houses and low-built adobes that Crockett remembered along Hackberry Creek. There was a bank now, made of bricks that must have been brought in by some big freight outfit. There were more saloons, too; he could make out at least three recently built ones on the south side of Pioneer.

It was a far cry from the straggling half-Spanish settlement he had known as a boy, the little more than shacks thrown up by the saloon people, gamblers and storekeepers to get the trade of the first cattlemen who settled this section of the territory. And it was a far cry from the small town where, more than five years ago, he'd been beaten by a mob for his Union sympathies, then driven out like a criminal.

Thinking of that he felt worry tighten his insides again, that same worry that had ridden cold and heavy with him since he'd left Kansas. In the saddle every day from sunup to dark, he'd controlled the fear that he'd meet someone who remembered, someone who might force a fight and start everything all over again.

Now, as he started King forward again, swinging wide to skirt a mesquite thicket, he stubbornly held in the worry with its edge of fear. He had the advantage, he was certain, coming back alone without anyone knowing.

Crockett rode slowly. He was large and deep-chested, of early middle age, the look of a tough and capable man on his copper-colored stubbled face. His denims and gray flannel shirt had a newness to them; still, they showed he had been on the trail a long time. His mount had carried him only past the edge of town before he became aware that he had no advantage, after all.

Men watched his approach from the entire length of Pioneer. They stood on the porches, boardwalks, some in the dusty streets, all staring. They sat on horses or in wagons and other rigs that filled the town. The tension that bounced from group to group was as real as the shimmering heat haze over the flat to the west.

Someone had spread the word he was returning, maybe one of the passengers or the driver on the stage that had passed him an hour back. Even despite the beard he'd grown, they'd recognized him. Whoever had told had done a good job, a damn good job.

Crockett's wide shoulders hunched slightly, his gray eyes narrowing. He held the gelding in with his knees, his right hand loose on the bridle, ready to drop down and back to his Colt if anyone challenged him.

One man had kept working—he could tell from the ringing of iron on iron as John Sutton pounded on his anvil. Staring ahead, he angled his mount to the left toward the blacksmith's shop. He pulled up the gelding in the wide work area in front of the open door, beside the big blacksmith.

"You got time to check my horse's shoes, John?" he said quietly.

Sutton looked up. He was a thick-chested man, with heavily muscled arms and huge thighs. The quick glance he allowed Crockett before he continued shaping a red-hot shoe said nothing.

"John," said Crockett in the same quiet voice, "do you have time to look at my horse?"

The blacksmith looked up again, but instead of speaking he stared over the gelding's rump at the street. From the corner of his eye Crockett saw a movement there. He swung smoothly around in the saddle, letting his hand drop down.

"Hello, Ruel."

Crockett's hand stopped when he saw the star of a town marshal. Hobart hadn't been large enough for a marshal before, but since Bol Taylor had been a county deputy, he was the natural choice for marshal. "Hello, Bol," Crockett answered.

The marshal, a tall and wiry man in his mid-forties, stood stiff-legged as he stared up at the rider. "You come here for trouble, Ruel?"

"No trouble. I only want John to check King's shoes. Maybe have his kid give him some water and a rub while I'm doing business."

Taylor spat a mouthful of tobacco juice as he glanced inside the barn. His eyes flicked over the horses in the stalls, then moved to the small corral beside the building. Four horses awaited the blacksmith's attention before he'd get to Crockett's. He noticed, too, that the watching men had begun to cross the street, slowly, uncertainly. John Sutton saw this and spoke for the first time.

"I'll take his horse next, Bol," he said.

"I can wait," said Crockett. "I'll wait my turn."

"I'll take your horse first," the huge blacksmith snapped. "I don't want any murderin' turncoat Texan in this town any longer than anybody else does."

Crockett's face showed nothing. He began to dismount, his eyes roaming beyond the marshal to the spectators. He heard someone snap a profane Spanish word, but gave it no notice. Most of the faces were familiar, especially the younger men who wore tattered remnants of Confederate uniforms, but none of the Allisons were present. Bob DeWitt and Harry Kelly were there. Both had been in on the beating.

Behind DeWitt the crowd suddenly opened up and a burly Federal soldier broke his way through to the clearing. He wore the yellow-lined breeches of the cavalry, with the stripes of a sergeant on his sleeve. He sized up Crockett with one glance.

"You having trouble with this man, Marshal?" He was perhaps thirty, and though he spoke to Taylor his eyes stayed on Crockett, first covering his face then dropping to the holstered Colt at his side. "He refuse to give up his gun?"

"No," answered Marshal Taylor. "He . . ."

"How come you're wearing that gun?" From the way the soldier disregarded the lawman it was clear that the matter was out of Taylor's hands.

"I didn't know there was a law against carrying a gun," Crockett said.

His eyes shifted, looking down the street to the front of one of the new buildings. A big man dressed in cowhand's clothing stood on the porch there, staring toward the crowd. He wore his gun in plain view, thonged down to his thigh. The sergeant glanced that way, then returned his look to Crockett.

"You damn Johnny Rebs," he snapped. Cursing loudly, he strode to the wide door of the blacksmith's shop and, with a metallic grating of rusty hinges, pushed it shut. There in bold black print was a weather-browned poster.

ATTENTION

As of today, guns or knives will not be allowed in Hobart. Everyone entering town will leave weapons at the livery stable, blacksmith shop or hotel. Weapons will be picked up again when leaving Hobart.

D. H. Cahoon, Lieutenant, U. S. Cavalry
March 10, 1866

The sergeant sneered. "Can you read, Reb?"

Crockett's face hardened. He saw the questioning expressions of the watchers close to him. He began unbuckling his gunbelt. "John can check my gun 'til I get back," he said.

Muttering broke out in the crowd, a low murmur that died instantly when the sergeant spoke. "You've got papers, Reb. Let me see them."

"I'm checking my guns," Crockett answered. "I'm obeying the law."

Again the sergeant swore hotly. "Don't answer me back, Reb. Let me see your papers!"

For a moment Crockett hesitated, glancing across the broad grass flat stretching out behind the corral, wishing he'd been smart enough to come in through the other side of town. Some of the onlookers pressed forward as he reached into the rear pocket of his denims and took out a folded envelope.

"My discharge, Sergeant," Crockett said crisply.

The soldier opened the envelope, then unfolded the contents. A sudden look of surprise came over his face. "Well, I'll be damned," he said. "Why didn't you say you were an officer with Meade?"

"Are you satisfied, Sergeant?"

"Yes, sir. . . . Say, we were with Meade at Cemetery Ridge." He grinned widely. "Remember that, Captain?"

Crockett was very much aware of the heavy hush that had settled over the listeners. He remembered the battle, remembered the thick heat after the April rain when Pickett's Virginians marched toward Cemetery Wall, dressed right and as tight-packed as this watching crowd. He remembered the slaughter that took place that April day, and how it had sickened him, just as this swaggering occupation soldier disgusted him now.

"My papers, Sergeant," he said.

"Yes, sir," the soldier said. He stared at the folded gunbelt and holster in Crockett's hand. As he passed the envelope back, he added, "You won't have to check that, Captain."

Crockett took the envelope, turned to the big blacksmith and offered the gun and belt. "I'll pick it up when I get my horse, John," he said.

Embarrassed by Crockett's snub the sergeant swung around at the watchers. "All right," he yelled. "Break it up. Get going there...."

The crowd began to disperse, a few of the younger men in threadbare gray stubbornly taking their time. Crockett could hear the sergeant still shouting as he turned away from the blacksmith.

Marshal Taylor put a restraining hand on Crockett's arm. "No trouble, Ruel," he said.

Crockett said quietly, "I've only got two stops to make, Bol. There'll be no trouble." Then, he cut across Pioneer toward the false-fronted general store.

The encounter with the Federal soldier had irritated him, although he'd known what he could expect in a town controlled by military occupation. He'd spent six months of postwar duty in Georgia as a Union officer and knew from experience the terrible indecencies of Reconstruction the South was undergoing, the corruption of the new political and financial powers, the injustices of the carpetbagger courts. Whenever he'd handled the business or affairs of the vanquished, he'd tried to be decent and fair, but he'd grown weary of banging his head against stone walls long before he'd been discharged. Partly because of this he'd come back alone, as would any man sick and tired of war and its consequences. The least he could hope for was that no one would connect him with any part of the occupation.

The sergeant had ruined any hope of that. Crockett had seen it in the eyes of every man in the crowd.

His high-heeled boots rang hollowly as he stepped from the dusty street onto the porch. Going inside the store, he closed the door gently, making certain it wouldn't slam. He'd waited years for this moment and could not afford to have anything go wrong.

He saw gray-haired Pitkin Allison immediately, a man of about sixty-five standing with his back to the door and talking with three women at the dry-goods counter. The storekeeper was coatless, and the sleeves of his white shirt were tucked under black garters.

Crockett waited until Allison had finished with the

sale. Then he walked past the counters, piled high with calicoes, boots and shoes, bandannas, pants and under-wear, to where the storekeeper stood.

At the sound of approaching footsteps Allison turned, and looked at Crockett. There was no trace of surprise on his wrinkled face.

"Thought you'd come in," Allison said, his gaze shifting from Crockett's face to the gunless hips and back to Crockett's eyes. "I won't have any fight with you."

"There's been too much fighting already, Mr. Allison. I wanted you to know that's how I feel. And what I said I . . ."

"All right," the storekeeper interrupted bluntly. "You've told it."

"I want Creed to know, too. He was the one I threatened. I'd like to talk it out with him."

Allison placed both hands palm-down on the counter, as if he were bracing himself. "You won't be talking anything out with Creed," he said in a low voice. "He was killed at Palmito Hill."

Crockett felt a sudden surge of emotion grip him, a mixture of pity for old Allison and the warmth of re-lief for himself. He said, "I'm sorry, Mr. Allison."

The storekeeper looked at him, saying nothing. In the silence that followed Crockett heard the sound of a door opening. Glancing to the left, he saw that a cowhand wearing a light homespun shirt and brown bullhide chaps stood in the doorway to the back room.

Allison saw the cowhand and spoke quickly. "Ben, you keep out of this."

"Why should I, Paw?" The cowhand stepped from the shadow of the doorway and came forward. He halted beneath the glare of an overhanging lamp. With a counter of dry goods between Crockett and himself, he could not see below Crockett's waist. "Your name Crockett?" he asked.

"Yes, that's my name."

"You're the murderin' turncoat Texan who got my brother drunk and then shot him."

Crockett said fast, hoarsely, "No. It wasn't that way, Ben."

Ben gestured as if to warn his father to keep clear. His eyes bore into Crockett. "Draw," he whispered coldly.

Crockett did not move. Allison told his son fast, "He came here to make peace, Ben. He . . ."

"Draw!" Ben Allison repeated. His cold stare was glued to Crockett, his right hand dropping a little lower.

"He hasn't got a gun, Ben!" his father yelled. "Don't shoot . . . don't!"

The cowhand's mouth dropped open in astonishment. "What?" he gasped.

Crockett said, "I came here to settle the trouble, not to make more."

Ben Allison strode forward, out of the glare of the lamplight. Now Crockett plainly saw the cowhand's youth. Although he had a stubble of beard he could be no more than eighteen.

Stopping five feet from Crockett, Ben said, "Get a gun. Get a gun and be out in the street yonder when . . ."

"No," his father said. "I've already lost two sons through senseless fighting." He started to move toward his son.

"Get a gun," Ben repeated to Crockett. His eyes had thinned to slits, and his mouth twitched.

His father was beside him now, and he grabbed Ben's right arm. "That's enough, Ben. . . . enough!"

Ben jerked his arm, but the gripping fingers only tightened. He swore, again tried to shake the hand free. The old storekeeper suddenly swung out, slapping his son's face violently.

"That's enough, Ben."

Stunned, the boy shot a pleading look at his father. "He killed Tom, Paw. Creed swore he'd gun him for it. I'm doin' what . . ."

"You'll do nothing," Allison yelled into Ben's face. He turned to look at Crockett and motioned with his free hand. "You better go."

Crockett stared into the old man's eyes, saw fear there. "All right," he said. He wheeled and headed for the door.

Ben's voice called after him. "Next time, you have a gun, Crockett. . . . Next time—" The words were cut off as the door closed behind Crockett.

Chapter Two

ONCE he was across Pioneer, Crockett halted. His hand trembled a little when he reached into his shirt pocket for the makings. There was a thick, sour taste in his mouth, and as he made the cigarette he spat to clear it. A boy, he thought dejectedly. Did I come all this way just to end up fighting a boy?

"Mister Crockett?"

The hail was close, friendly. Turning, Crockett saw it was spoken by a tall, spidery man of about his own age. He wore a soft black fedora and was immaculately dressed in an expensive gray suit that broke correctly over his polished shoes. In the bright glare of the sunshine he stood out like a fashion plate among the ragged Texans lounging on the porches.

Smiling, the man offered his hand. "My name is Howells, Mister Crockett . . . William F. Howells."

Crockett nodded, took the man's hand. Eight months ago he'd received a letter from this Howells, a banker, telling of his father's death from pneumonia. "I was just going over to see you," he said. "I appreciate everything you did for us last winter."

"I was glad to do what I could," Howells said seriously. "I have all the papers in my office if you'd like to clear it up now."

Nodding, Crockett walked toward the new brick building that housed the bank. Beside him, Howells said, "I was fortunate to find a buyer so quickly, considering how things are."

"A buyer?" Crockett said.

"Yes. I found a stockman who'll pay ten thousand for your land. I wrote you about it."

Crockett hesitated at the bottom of the bank steps. He dropped his cigarette, ground it out in the dust with his boot heel. "I never got that letter, Mr. Howells. I was going in to see you about a loan."

Howells' smooth thin face showed surprise. "Well, I don't know," he began, but his voice fell off as he noticed a handsomely dressed woman walking toward them. His look returned to Crockett. "Have you talked to your brother about this?"

"I haven't seen Johnny since sixty-one, Mr. Howells."

"But he talked to me about selling," Howells told him. "He was only waiting until you came back, so you'd get your share of the money."

Crockett halted just inside the bank lobby and glanced back along the porches. "Look at all these men loafing, Mr. Howells," he said. "They're out of work because there're no jobs for them. If we sold our spread, we'd be sitting there with them."

The banker wet his lips, seeming not quite sure what to say. The woman he had noticed reached them now and stopped. She was a startlingly lovely brunette, tall and finely shaped, and, Crockett guessed, in her late twenties. Her clothes, from flowered hat to flowing blue skirt, were the latest New York fashion. As Howells was representative of the wealthy carpetbagger men, she was typical of their women.

"My sister," Howells said. "Marion, Mr. Ruel Crockett."

Crockett touched the wide brim of his sombrero. "Miss Howells," he said.

Marion Howells smiled. "William tells me you've just come from the East," she said. "We must have you in for dinner, Mr. Crockett."

"Not the East, Miss Howells. I left Georgia almost two months ago."

"Well, after our business is finished, we can . . ." Howells stopped talking at the sound of a door opening in the far end of the lobby.

The man who had come out of the banker's office was tall, over six feet, with a wide, thick body fitted perfectly to his finely tailored brown broadcloth. He looked at the woman as if surprised she was present.

"I thought you called me over here to do business," the man said to Howells.

"We are, Mister Gould," the banker answered quickly. "Marion just stopped for a minute." He stared at his sister.

Marion Howells' eyebrows lifted slightly. A strange tenseness had come over her. She seemed purposely to be keeping her eyes from Gould as she spoke.

"Perhaps we'll be able to see you soon, Mr. Crockett. We're at the hotel." Her gaze shifted to Gould then, bold and challenging, as she went to the door and closed it behind her.

In a strained voice Howells said to Crockett, "This is Franklin Gould. I mentioned he was interested in buying your ranch."

Gould said, "I'm a busy man, Crockett. I'd like to clear up the sale right away."

Crockett's eyes measured the prosperous-looking man. There was no sign of the real stockman here, only the typical and obvious confidence of the carpetbagger Unionist.

"I have no intention of selling my ranch," he said.

Gould glanced at Howells. "I'd been told you had. And I thought ten thousand was a generous figure." From the way his tone had softened, it was clear that it was in Howells' hands now.

"You couldn't buy my place for twice that price," said Crockett. He turned away from Gould, added to Howells, "Do we talk about that loan or not?"

"Well ... I ..." The banker's eyes flicked to Gould. The stockman had seated himself in a chair beneath a large double frame holding portraits of Abraham Lincoln and General Grant. Crossing his legs, Gould took a cigar from his pocket and began unwrapping it. Howells said, "Well ... yes. What had you planned on?"

"Two thousand."

Howells nodded. "That isn't too much for us," he said. "I'll have to know about collateral first."

"Diamond C is all I have right now, besides my horse and personal belongings. But the scrip my father turned over to you is worth ten times what I need."

The banker began to shake his head. "You can't use mortgaged property as collateral."

"I know that," Crockett said firmly. He could tell what was going on here from the way Gould sat back, smoking confidently. But he held down his irritation, calming his voice. "Mr. Howells, when I was discharged I was told I rated extra time to pay off my debts caused by the war. I intend to do just that through a loan. Now, do I get it here, or do I have to ride down to Gonzales?"

"Well . . . I'll have to check into your status."

"How long will that take?"

"A day or two. I can telegraph through the army authorities in Austin—"

Gould broke in from where he sat. "Those cattle on the range, Crockett," he said. "They don't all belong to you."

"It's open range," Crockett said quietly. "With all the war-neglected stock, there's more than enough for everybody."

"But very few have your brand."

Crockett stared directly at the stockman. "The herd I put on the trail will all have my brand. You can be sure of that."

Uncrossing his legs, Gould stood. "I own land here, Crockett. I for one wouldn't want you branding any cows that belong to me."

A tense hardness rode his voice, a tone that was loud in the quiet lobby. Behind Gould the office door swung back, and a huge cowhand whose chest bulged out of his rumpled clothing stepped into the room. He glared at Crockett from under his flat-crowned hat, waited for Gould to say something.

"Selling now would save you trouble over those cows," Gould said flatly.

"I don't want trouble," Crockett said. "But I don't run easy if it comes. I start mavericking as soon as I can." He paid no attention to the newcomer, keeping his hard eyes on Gould for a few moments, finally shifting to the banker.

"I'll be back in two days," he added. "You let me know what you decide." Then he turned and walked from the lobby.

Before the door closed behind him the cowhand started

ahead, his massive weight creaking the floor. But a simple gesture from Gould stopped him. Gould puffed slowly on his cigar, spoke through ropy layers of smoke. "So that's that," he said. "I gave him his chance."

"I did the best I could," Howells offered uneasily. "I couldn't come right out and say no to a loan."

Gould's hand waved him silent. As he blew the heavy smoke away from his face, he looked at the well-built cowhand.

"Jason, give Crockett time to clear town. Then, ride out and get Brazos."

Howells stared at Gould. "No . . . no more killing," he said quickly. "There are two brothers out there. And Limpy. You can't . . ."

"You'd rather have Crockett keep his place?" Gould snapped. "Don't you realize you can hang ten years from now just as fast as today?"

"I don't want any more killing. I'd rather quit."

Gould swore at him. "You can't quit." He became quiet again, rubbing his smooth jaw for several moments. Shortly, he said, "You just get the papers ready for me on Crockett's property."

"But Crockett's a Union vet. He has rights the Rebels we've been dealing with haven't got."

Again Gould swore. "Forget his rights," he said emphatically. "Brazos and Jason are going out there tomorrow. We'll see how uneasy this Crockett has to get before he runs."

"I can't do that," Howells said. "There are laws. I have to . . ."

"Howells," said Gould, "get the papers—now."

The interruption made the banker pause. He was silent, considering the sharp words. He shook his head hopelessly, then went around behind the desk and opened the middle drawer.

Crockett waited in the shade of the cottonwood behind the blacksmith's shop, smoking one cigarette after another until Sutton finished with his horse. The big blacksmith said nothing while Crockett paid him and then mounted. None of the men along the street spoke to him as he rode past. They simply stared as they had been doing and continued to watch him until he cut back onto the dusty wagon road going south.

Disappointment rode with Crockett. He'd come into Hobart in the hope that he could make peace with some of those he had left in hate. Instead, he'd made more enemies. Now that he was back again on the open flat he was glad to leave Hobart behind.

He rode slowly so King wouldn't tire under the driving heat of the afternoon sun, following Hackberry Creek at first to give the animal the benefit of shade from the timber lining the water's edge.

To the southeast, toward his own land, the gentle, rolling cow country of Choctaw Flats ran for a good ten miles before the distant treeline blotted from view the prairie beyond. Here and there mesquite thickets stretched out for miles, tall cactuses rose up in spots among the twisted thorny trees.

One-hundred yards below Hobart he passed the Army encampment. Just beyond that was a pleasant grassy hollow, shaded by a plentiful landscape of timber. In this hollow was a large, partially constructed house with a barn behind it. From the skeletal structure already completed, Crockett could see it would be a mansion matching any of the fine plantation houses he'd seen throughout the South.

Crockett reined to the right to cross the log wagon bridge that had been built when he was a boy. It was shady, secluded amid a copse of moss-hung water oaks spotted with hackberry. On the west bank he pulled in to allow King a last drink before returning to the shimmering heat of the prairie.

The horse sensed the men before Crockett saw them. His head came up fast, his ears poking forward. Ten feet to the right, where the brush thickened along the creek's bank, four men had stepped out from behind the wide trunks of the oaks.

More men appeared on the other side of the bridge. Both groups closed together, blocking Crockett's path. He sat quietly, looking from one man to another, recognizing most of them. None of the eight carried a gun; all wore at least one faded article of gray clothing, telling Crockett they were all Confederate veterans. One of them, a short, bantam-legged man with thick red hair and beard, stepped forward.

"You remember me, Crockett?" he asked brazenly. A snicker of amusement came from the others, but that was silenced when Crockett spoke.

"Bob DeWitt . . . you used to work for Jim Cox's outfit."

"Wal, ain't that nice," DeWitt said pointedly. "The bluebelly remembers us, boys. Wonder if he remembers the party we gave him 'fore he went away?"

He swaggered a few steps closer. The others fell in behind. This was the same kind of mob that had closed in on Crockett five years before, the same kind that had beaten him senseless and sent him back to his father's ranch half alive. Crockett's right hand dropped to the round of his thigh, a few inches from his gun.

"Don't git spooked," DeWitt said amiably. "We jest wanna talk to you."

"You didn't wait here just to talk."

DeWitt nodded and turned to look back at his followers. "I'll say we didn't, did we, you Johnny Rebs? We got no stomach for talkin' t' turncoat Texans, do we?"

A murmur of assent came then, punctuated by a few blasphemies and angry remarks. DeWitt reached up and took hold of the claybank's bridle.

"You fought a long time fer them Yankees, Crockett," he said. "You must be a heap proud of what your carpetbagger friends are doin' t' Texas."

"Let go that bridle," Crockett said. He began backing the gelding.

DeWitt held on, despite the power of the horse's head pulling up hard to force him to let go. A loud chorus of angry yells broke out. "Grab him," a voice called. "We'll give him what we gave him for killin' Tom Allison," cried another. "Drag him down," shouted a third, cursing.

Crockett felt them pressing in all around him. Arms and hands reached for him, clawed at him, as the yelling rose to lynch-mob pitch. One hand got hold of Crockett's leg, and he felt himself being yanked, jerked from the saddle.

Chapter Three

FEAR of what lay in the fury of the mob welled up in Crockett, and with fear came strength. He swung his fist violently, landing a solid blow on the man who pulled at his leg, sending him sprawling. Straightening in the saddle, he socked his spurs to the claybank, yanked the horse's head up wildly, tearing the bridle from DeWitt's fingers.

Crockett's foot shot out, the boot smashing into the face of a man who'd reached up to catch him about the waist. DeWitt slid in close to the saddle and tried to pluck the Colt from its holster. Crockett's hand streaked back, gripped the weapon's butt. He swung it high and brought it down on the thick mass of red hair. As he jabbed the spurs into the gelding again, he felt the impact of the blow run up his arm, saw DeWitt's scalp split and blood gush from the laceration.

Whinnying painfully from the shock of the spurs, the horse whirled, kicking as he started his forward lunge. A hoof caught an attacker along the right leg, and the man screamed in agony.

All but one of the attackers in close dove out of the path of the charging animal. Daringly, the lone figure pivoted to the side as the horse bolted past, then tried to grab at Crockett in a last desperate effort to unsaddle him.

Crockett's left arm swung down, hitting the back of the cowhand's head, throwing him down face-first in the dust. Crockett let the gelding go until he was clear of the mob. Then, he reined in hard, swinging the animal around so he could face the men and watch for another assault.

But the fight was gone from the attackers. Two men bent over the inert form of DeWitt. The man whom Crockett had kicked rose unsteadily to his feet. The collison with the boot had done his face little good. His nose and mouth were split, and blood seeped down to his skinned chin.

Still dazed, he began to rage, charging for Crockett.

"Hold him!" rasped Crockett. Two men started following him, moving as if they were joining the charge. "Hold him!" Crockett repeated. "Get back . . . don't try beating me again!"

The two men grabbed hold of their comrade and held him. The man stared ahead like a drunk, his eyes focused hatefully on Crockett.

"Get out, get out!" he screamed. "Get out!"

For a few moments Crockett stared down at the angry faces in silence. Slowly he holstered the Colt. "Don't ever try beating me . . . don't ever try it again." His voice was tense, hard.

He turned the gelding and started toward the flat at a gallop.

Behind him there was heavy quiet. The men returned to where DeWitt lay. They stood without speaking while the redheaded cowhand came around and groggily pushed himself up onto one elbow. Tenderly he brushed his hand across his hair and looked at the blood-smeared palm.

He stared blankly at the bloody hand for a long moment, then raised his eyes to the others.

"I'll kill him," he muttered. "I'll kill him."

Well clear of the trees now, Crockett slowed the gelding, letting the animal make his own pace in the heat. Reaction still made his stomach tremble, still held the brackish taste of nausea in his mouth. He gulped in slow breaths of air, fighting himself to control his body and nerves.

Three hours of steady riding passed. He moved faster once beyond the northern boundary of Diamond C. He knew this cactus- and mesquite-fringed expanse of range like the back of his hand—every dip and swell and clump of timber south to where the rougher and brushier terrain began, and west to the Llano and San Saba, almost clear to the Comanche country bordering the Staked Plain.

Twilight's dark blanket had begun to settle over the prairie by the time Crockett sighted his home. He first saw the grove of live oaks shading the spring that had made Theodore Crockett decide to settle here so many years ago. Soon the individual buildings were clear, and it was apparent in the darkening light that things had deteriorated here. The squat adobe building that had been the bunkhouse showed ugly gaping scars where great pieces had fallen off its walls. Two broken windows were unrepaired in the log-and-adobe main house. The roof of the barn sagged. Only the pole and rawhide corral showed signs of having been repaired, at a break near the gate.

Yet there was no feeling of depression in Crockett. He'd seen much worse ruins than this all through the invalid South. He kneed the claybank and rode up the small knoll that held the house.

He was halfway up the rise when Johnny appeared in the doorway. Johnny was an inch or so shorter than his brother, but his shoulders were heavier. The war hadn't aged him. He seemed years younger than twenty-nine, with his blond hair and stubble of beard, soft and light like the hair on his arms. He stood quietly until Crockett reached him. "Johnny, boy. You sure look good."

"Been all right, Ruel. How are you?" His voice was neutral, neither friendly nor unfriendly.

"Good, John," said Crockett, sensing that his brother felt as awkward at this moment as he did. He glanced around while he dismounted. "Place certainly needs work."

"It was a hard war here, Ruel," Johnny answered pointedly.

Nodding, Crockett was silent. His gaze moved behind the house to the small cemetery that had held their mother since a Comanche raid in fifty-one. Now, two gravestones rose up there, side by side in the evening shadows.

"You cut a stone for Pa," Crockett said, his words quiet.

"Fred Hardin put it up, Ruel. He had it up when I got back."

"Fred's still around here?"

Johnny nodded his head and, after a quick glance over his shoulder at the prairie, said, "Put up your horse and come on inside."

Crockett stared at him. Johnny was never one to camouflage his emotions; worry, possibly fear, was mirrored clearly in his honest eyes. "Why the rush, Johnny?"

"Rube Mitchell got shot right after he got back. Came near gettin' killed, Ruel."

Staring at him, Crockett swallowed. Mitchell had been another of the Hobart County men who'd gone north to fight for the Union.

"I'll be in in a little while," he said.

He tended to his horse, and by the time he got to the house Johnny had already lighted the coal-oil table lamp. He looked around from the conical Mexican fireplace. "Wash up while I fix somethin'," he said, nodding to the water-filled basin beneath the pump.

"Sure." Crockett smiled and began unbuttoning his shirt. The room's furnishings—from worn throw rugs to rawhide-bottomed chairs, oak table and wall cabinet, all simple and plain articles for utility—were covered by a deep layer of dust. Crockett wiped the top of a chair clean before laying down his shirt.

He was moving the basin from beneath the pump when he realized Johnny was watching him. He glanced at his brother.

Johnny stared at him, his big chest rising and falling rapidly. "Where'd you get that, Ruel?"

Unconsciously, Crockett ran his fingers over the jagged scar running the length of the ribs on his right side.

"Chickamauga," he answered.

For a few moments, Johnny was silent. Finally, he said seriously, "I wasn't there, Ruel."

Looking at him Crockett thought, He hasn't changed at all. And, with his kid brother, it meant the war wouldn't keep a breach between them. Johnny's hate would be mainly on the circumstances of a Civil War that would make brother fight brother. "I was told you wanted to sell out here," he said.

"Not that I want . . . I figured it would be best to."

"Because of me?"

" 'Cause of everythin'. The way the Unionists and carpetbaggers have Texas tied up, even a spread this size hasn't got a chance. There's no money, not even of Mexican make, and there's no market for our beef. I figgered ten thousand is a mighty fair price, 'specially when they can get the place for taxes anyway."

"Where would you go, Johnny?" Crockett took a sack towel and began wiping his face and shoulders.

"California, mebe," Johnny said shortly. "Up to the gold stakes in Montana. Mebe stay here in Hobart for awhile."

"You're a cattle man, Johnny. You belong here, the same as I do." He gestured at the night outside, the circular sweep of his arm taking in the whole prairie. "There's five years of war-neglected herd out there. We could clear enough before next year to pay off anything we owe the bank."

Johnny looked at him hopefully. But, just as quickly, his face fell. "Pa turned over all his scrip to the bank," he said. "Mortgage is overdue now, Ruel. We . . ."

"We can get a loan." He dropped the soggy towel into the basin and crossed to the fireplace. "Look, Johnny. Let me handle the loan. But whatever I get we owe together. We'll split everything down the middle like we used to."

His brother looked at him in silence. Then, he walked to the door and stared out into the night, as if he was watching for something.

"There's a market in the north for all the beef we can get on the trail," Crockett told him. "A man named Joe McCoy is building a new railhead in Abilene. It's just waiting for Texas beef. There are yards for cattle, a hotel—everything. We can round up enough to make our first drive this fall."

"That's a long trail. And up through the Nations besides."

"No worry there, Johnny. I took my time coming down, scouting all the way. There's plenty of water if we drive right. We can bribe the Comanches with a few head of beef, more if they want it. It's only a little more than a thousand miles at most. We can . . ."

"Who are you going to get to work this drive? You think any cowhand down here'll ride for you?"

"That's where you come in, Johnny. You'll be trail boss. I'll ride for you."

Again Johnny was silent, still watching the darkness. In the quiet Crockett took the makings from his shirt pocket and began rolling a cigarette. The prairie wind whistling through a crack in the wall broke the stillness. Outside, somewhere on the moonlit range, the warbling call of a night bird sounded.

Johnny said finally, "Once we cross the Colorado and the Brazos, it'd be clear travelin' right to the Red."

"Right." Crockett moved closer to the fireplace. "We'll hire four hands and start mavericking tomorrow. Sutton can make up running irons for us in a couple hours."

Bobbing his head, Johnny echoed, "In the morning." Then, he was thoughtful again, as if pondering something inscrutable. "I'm glad, Ruel," he added shortly. "I figger Pa would've wanted us to stay."

"I figured that, too," Crockett said.

They had just started eating when Crockett heard the low sounds of horses and the squeaking of a vehicle. Johnny stood quickly, went to the door. Stepping behind his brother, Crockett saw that a girl was driving the approaching buggy. The horseman with her was Clint Hollis from the Bar 7. In the moonlight Crockett could see little of the girl, only that she was slender and light-haired, holding her shoulders squared as she pulled the bay gelding to a halt.

"Who is she?" Crockett asked.

"Janet Bankhead . . . my girl," Johnny said a bit awkwardly.

The name was not familiar to Crockett. "She's new to this county."

"Yes. She came with her father from Kentucky. Since he died, she's worked for Pitkin Allison. Mae Hollis's been sick, so she rode down to help a coupla days. Good woman, Ruel."

Crockett sensed the tone of pride in his brother's words. "I know that," he said, gripping Johnny's arm, tightening his fingers and letting go quickly as he had when they were young.

Grinning at him, Johnny said, "I'll have them come in for a bite."

"You don't have to, Johnny."

"You're my brother, Ruel," Johnny told him. "I'll ask them in."

Crockett followed him outside. A warmth coursed through him because of his brother's words, but the feeling lacked completeness. He hadn't planned on a girl, hadn't even dreamed one existed. Yet, with Johnny being so serious about her, she'd have to be considered in what they did from here on.

"Hey, I expected you earlier," Johnny called as he got close to the buggy.

The girl smiled pleasantly at him. "We got a late start," she said, standing, ready to get down.

Johnny said, "This is my brother Ruel, Janet. Ruel, this is Janet." He gestured towards the rider. "Ruel, you know Clint Hollis."

The rider's head bobbed up and down, but he did not look at Crockett. "I'll be gittin' back," he said. "Obliged, Janet."

Janet nodded. She sat again as Johnny said, "Come in, both of you. We got steak on."

"No, my woman'll need me," the rider said, and he began turning his mount. Janet watched him go, then looked at Johnny. "It's late. Mr. Allison will be worried."

In the short silence that fell over the yard, Crockett studied the woman. He saw right away that she was older than his brother, thirty-three or thirty-four, with a softness of skin that didn't hide the serious lines of her face. Her mature features had a quiet beauty to them, but it was her eyes that held Crockett. They were very lovely, deeply blue, with a steadiness that seemed to return his appraisal.

"You don't mind if I ride in now?" Johnny said. "I'll get them riders out at sunup so we can start work early."

"You go ahead," Crockett told him.

Johnny turned and walked toward the barn. Crockett

saw that for some reason Janet had tensed as she watched him go, and to offset the feeling she sat forward a little, her back straight, raising her left hand unconsciously to smooth her bodice. In that motion, Crockett saw the large gold band on her finger.

Her eyes shifted to his face, and he quickly lifted his gaze, feeling the color rise to his cheeks. She watched him gravely.

"You changed Johnny's mind about the ranch," she said.

"Yes. There's no sense selling, not with the opportunity we have."

She said flatly, "There isn't much opportunity these days in Texas."

"There is if you work at it." He spoke more curtly than he had intended and instantly regretted it. He realized now he'd held some resentment for her meddling in affairs which were strictly the province of Johnny and himself. "With the war over," he said gently, "we should look ahead."

"That's easy for you to say."

He didn't understand this. "I believe a man has to keep working."

She had paled, and her lower lip trembled. "Have you seen all the men loafing in Hobart?" she asked defiantly. "They are men who'd like to keep on trying, but the war broke their spirits. You wouldn't know about that, how it is to have defeat and mistreatment eating away at you. There's nothing wrong with your spirit because ..."

"The war's over," he cut in. "The sooner it's forgotten, the sooner all of us will get back to normal. You, too, Janet."

"Normal," she said slowly. "With my husband killed at Shiloh ... and my father dead soon after from heartbreak."

"I didn't know," he began, but Johnny was leading his black toward them and Crockett stopped. She turned her face away from him, then waited quietly while Johnny tied the horse behind the buggy and climbed up beside her.

"I'll be back by sunup," Johnny said, glancing at his

brother. "You want four hands for now. And running irons, right?"

"Four, that's right." Crockett stood motionless as they drove away together into the quiet darkness. He stared after them, a frown on his face, then began rolling a cigarette.

She had a hold over Johnny, all right. It was probably Janet who had had the idea of selling Diamond C. If she kept this up, she could cause trouble. He'd have to move everything along faster, beginning with the loan. He'd get his cowhands started in the morning, then go back to town by night and get the financial problem solved right away.

Chapter Four

CROCKETT slept soundly that night for the first time since coming down the long trail from Abilene. He rose before daylight, shaved and washed, shivering slightly in the pre-dawn chill. After finishing a hasty breakfast, he went outside to take care of King.

All trace of darkness had faded, slowly giving way to the blue and cloudless sky of daybreak. The rusty hinges creaked loudly as Crockett pulled back the barn door. A noisy scuffling came from inside, and in the shadowy light filtering into the building he saw old Fred Hardin. The white-haired horse wrangler was just sitting up on a pile of straw he'd evidently used as a bed last night. His boney, wrinkled face was strained, tense as he stared at Crockett.

"Fred . . ." Crockett said. Going forward, he held out his hand. "Good to see you, Fred."

Hardin's face lost the frightened look. He visibly wet his lips as he stood unsteadily and took a stiff-legged step toward Crockett. A bronc-busting accident had crippled him twenty-odd years before, but despite his limp he'd been kept on by Theodore Crockett. A reeking smell of raw whisky followed him, making it clear his unsteadiness wasn't just a game leg.

"Heard you was back, Ruel," he said. "Heard it last night in town." He made no motion to shake, but lifted an unsteady hand and rubbed his mouth.

Crockett was confused. He'd known the man since Hardin had taught him to ride as a boy. He'd never been a heavy drinker, not even after he hurt his leg.

"Well, Fred," Crockett said, "I can see you're glad to have me back."

"No, Ruel. It ain't that." He shook Crockett's hand awkwardly. "I'm danged glad you're back. I'm jest sorry your Paw ain't . . ."

"Thanks for taking care of the grave, Fred. You were good to do that."

Fred Hardin's face stiffened and he began to breathe heavier. "I didn't do nothin'."

"Johnny and I think you did, Fred. We . . ."

"I didn't do nothin'." Hardin waved an unsteady hand into the air. When it fell, he reached into his back pocket and took out a bottle. "Don't tell me I did anythin' extra," he said. "Not after how good your Paw was to me."

Crockett was silent as Hardin drank, tilting the bottle high to get a mouthful. When he swallowed, he looked away from Crockett and limped back to his straw bed. "I wanna sleep," he said. "Lemme 'lone so I c'n . . ."

Hesitating, the white-haired old man dropped the whisky bottle, then cocked his head, listening. Crockett caught the clomping of horses approaching on the hard pan to the east. Hardin half-ran to the door, stared out, the intense look of fear back on his face.

"Them riders," he asked. "What they want?"

Through the doorway Crockett counted five horsemen, Johnny in the lead. He recognized the Johnson brothers and Bill Fauna. The last he knew only by sight but remembered he was called Little Joe. "That's our new crew, Fred," he said. "We're going out mavericking."

It took a few moments for the statement to penetrate Hardin's liquor-muddled brain. "You're gonna bring stock back here?"

Nodding, Crockett answered, "And we're making **a**

trail drive this fall.'' He watched the bleary eyes grow doubtful, then added, ''I'd say ten, maybe eleven riders'll make the drive. How many mounts will we need in a remuda?''

''Six . . . seven horses for each man,'' Hardin said.

''Okay. We want you to get busy on them. You'll have plenty of time to . . .''

''Money?'' Hardin said, cutting in. ''Where'll you get the money?''

''We're getting a loan.'' Crockett turned, started away, then stopped. ''You get the bunkhouse cleaned up for the crew. And move your own things in with John and me, Fred.''

Crockett walked from the barn. Into his mind came a picture of the Fred Hardin of twenty years ago. A friendly, ambitious cowhand, never drunk, capable in everything he did. Now the big question was just how far down he'd gone, if there was any chance of helping him.

Johnny had dismounted. ''You ready to go?'' he said.

''How about breakfast?'' asked Crockett.

''We spent the night at Chino and Flora Woffard's place. Ate early,'' Johnny told him. ''But we can stand some coffee.''

He motioned to the cowhands, and they began to dismount. None looked at Crockett, who glanced from face to face. He'd hoped his hiring them would establish some slight bond of kinship between them and himself. Still keeping their eyes from him in withdrawn silence, they went as a group toward the house. Johnny turned and started after them, but Crockett's hand on his arm stopped him.

''I just saw Fred in the barn, John. How long has he been like that?''

''Since before I got back, anyway.''

''He's been that bad?''

''Just steady drinkin','' Johnny said. ''He won't say anythin' . . . won't even come inside here to sleep. He jest stays out there in the barn. I figger maybe he started drinkin' after Pa died.''

''Yes,'' Crockett said, frowning. ''That could be it. You take care of the men, John. I'll saddle King.''

Johnny noticed the frown. "Ruel," he said, "one thing I want straight. We stick here, Fred stays too—no matter what he's like."

Crockett merely nodded. He was thinking of when he'd first seen the old cowhand in the barn. The expression on Hardin's face had been too much like terror to be simply the result of a startled awakening.

Fred Hardin watched the Crockett brothers talking, a queer expression on his wrinkled face. Then, while Ruel led King out and saddled him, the old man stood there, absently scratching his stubbled beard, an upsurge of hope tingling inside him. Finally, he swung around and walked back to his straw bed.

He felt a craving in his throat, an aching for one more swallow of whisky, but he did not pick up the half-filled bottle lying on the hay. Instead, he shoved the tail of his shirt into his waistband and began gathering his belongings.

By the time the squeal of leather and jingling of spurs came from the yard, telling him that the Crocketts and the crew were mounting, he'd completely cleaned up the area he'd used as a bedroom for so long.

When the riders headed out onto the flat, he went to the door and watched until they were just small blobs far out beneath the rapidly-heating morning sun. Almost like the old days when Ted Crockett was alive, he thought as he returned to his work. He felt good, useful. It had been such a long time since he'd felt this way.

He finished in the barn, then walked with his limping gait to the adobe bunkhouse and began cleaning it. He knew he could never bring himself to go back and live inside the main house, but he'd be happy living within these gypsum walls. After all the time in the barn, it was good to look forward to being out of the heat in summer and the terrible prairie wind in winter. He was so busy with hand and mind that he didn't hear the riders come into the yard. But he recognized the voice of Brazos Helm yelling to him.

"Limpy! Get out here!"

Fred Hardin's body stiffened. Wildly, he looked around, seeking a place to hide.

"Get out here, Limpy," the rough voice called once more. Quick talk went on outside. The sound of a man climbing down from the saddle followed.

Boots clumped towards the doorway, and the massive body of Jason Dobey blocked out the light.

"You was told to come out, Limpy," Jason said, his voice penetrating the stillness. "You ain't hidin' 'cause you been doin' any talkin'?"

Hurriedly, Hardin limped forward. "No . . . no, I haven't said a word, Jason. I wouldn't say nothin', Jason."

Once he was out in the hot sunlight the huge cowhand grabbed his arm and pushed him forward, toward where Brazos sat his black horse.

Brazos Helm, a tall, bewhiskered man, eased his mount forward, his hard eyes fastened on Hardin's face. "What you doin', Limpy?"

"Givin' the bunkhouse a good cleanin'." He stared at the big Starr .44 tied to Brazos' leg, surprised to hear the strength in his own voice.

The tall rider halted, his heavy features not changing as he chuckled. "Now, why would the Crockett boys be fixin' a bunkhouse?"

"They hired riders an' gone maverickin'. They . . ."

"Maverickin' . . . on Mr. Gould's land?"

"Ruel said he was gettin' a loan."

"Gould's gonna get this land." He shifted his weight in the saddle. "You knew that all along now, didn't you, amigo?"

Both men watched Hardin. The giant seemed amused, but Brazos glowered.

"You knew that all along," Brazos repeated. "And you was plannin' on leavin' here, wasn't you, amigo?"

"You can't . . ." The old man began waving his arms, but Jason's powerful right arm grabbed his shoulder, held him. The free hand swung out, slapped the white head hard, knocking Hardin to the dirt.

Brazos stared down at the prostrate man. "You was leavin'."

Jason's boot came off the ground, aimed to strike. Hardin swallowed. His voice rose in a pleading shriek.

"I'll go . . . I'll go!" He scrambled away on all fours like a beaten dog.

Brazos chuckled. "You remember I'm stayin' around, amigo," he said flatly. He nodded to Jason, added, "You ride back and tell Gould I'm goin' after them maverickers."

The huge cowhand mounted, and the two riders swung their mounts and went from the yard. Fred Hardin rose to his feet slowly. Groggily, he walked to the barn. Once inside, he dared to look out, saw that the riders had stopped to talk and water their horses at the spring in the oak grove.

Hardin watched until Jason turned back toward town and Brazos headed south. He exhaled with a hopeless, whining noise. Then, he went to the hay bin and picked up the bottle that lay there. He took a long drink, wheezing and grunting for air, finishing the whisky.

Chapter Five

THE DIAMOND C CREW worked in teams, the Johnson boys starting in the rolling pastures at the west boundary and working east, and Fauna and Little Joe taking the rougher and brushier country to the southeast. The morning was hot, the sun beating down fiercely. Crockett rode hard, worked hard from the first moment he and Johnny came on some long-horned cattle drifting toward a spring a quarter mile south of the ranch buildings.

They put their own brand on eleven cows before the early morning shadows began shortening beneath their moving horses. Two more old cows that Theodore Crockett must have branded were found among some stock they struck an hour before they sighted Fauna and Little Joe at ten.

Fauna was cooking two wild turkeys he'd shot over the cow chip branding fire, while Little Joe was finishing with a bawling yearling steer. Little Joe, a small, pudgy man, waved and walked to where the Crocketts had reined in.

"That's number nine." He spoke to Johnny only, as if he were alone.

Johnny started to dismount. "With ours, that's twenty-two. Not a bad start at all."

Crockett nodded and began climbing down. He heard Fauna's invitation to share the turkeys, but still felt the cowhands' blunt attitude.

"Little Joe says they saw four head Pa branded," Johnny told him. "That's close to thirty already."

Hunkering down, Crockett filled and lighted his pipe, took a few silent puffs. "There's enough stock on this range for every cowman in the county," he said finally. "When you go past the Waggoner spread stop in and tell them what we're doing. The Colliers, too. We get enough of a gather, maybe we can make it one big drive."

Little Joe made no reply to that. He spat a mouthful of tobacco juice and handed Crockett a good-sized piece of turkey.

Taking it, Crockett said nothing. It was enough to know the ice was broken, if only momentarily. He did not join in the small talk and said little while he ate, gnawing the bones clean and swallowing some steaming coffee before returning to his pipe.

When they finished eating, Crockett said to Little Joe, "Drive what you brand back to the house. I want some cattle there so people will know we're working." Then, to Johnny, "We'll ride into town and get the loan straightened out."

His brother grinned. "I won't hold you back, boy. I've got more'n one stop in Hobart."

The wide lobby of the bank was much cooler than the street. A town woman wearing a blue calico dress stood at the teller's window. Behind the window the mustached teller was talking to Howells. The banker was so engrossed in the conversation he did not notice the Crockett brothers until they halted behind the woman.

Howells' gaze moved absently to them, away, and almost instantly back to Crockett's face. Surprised, he said, "Mr. Crockett?"

Crockett's voice was quiet. "We thought we'd come in about the loan."

"But I thought you were on the range. I thought you were coming back tomorrow."

"We had to change our plans."

"Well . . ." The banker shifted uncomfortably, nodded at the woman. "Do you mind waiting until I'm through with Mrs. Simmons?"

"No, we don't mind."

He and Johnny went to a bench at the far end of the lobby and sat. Crockett hadn't liked Howells' deceptive actions, nor did he like the way the banker was leaning close to the teller now, head cocked and talking fast.

Howells took over the transaction with the woman, smiling as he spoke to her. The clerk busied himself with some papers at the desk. Crockett watched them, not quite sure something wasn't wrong. But any doubt left him when he saw the clerk get up and, appearing to be searching for something, open the back door and go out.

Then Crockett returned to the iron-barred teller's window and stood behind the woman.

While Howells worked, he watched Crockett from the corner of his eye. Finally, he stamped a paper and handed it to the woman. "I hope to see you next week, Mrs. Simmons," he said. Then he looked at Crockett. "You asked about the loan?"

"That's what we're here for."

Howells swallowed, glancing over Crockett's shoulder. He laid the pen he held carefully on the window ledge, cleared his throat. "I don't know about the money, Mr. Crockett. You don't have . . ."

"Yes or no, Mr. Howells? If not, I'll ride right down to Gonzales." Behind him, Crockett heard Johnny get noisily to his feet and stomp through the lobby.

The banker's eyes flicked to Johnny and back to Crockett. "You d—don't have collateral," he sputtered. "I couldn't lend money without collateral."

"What is this?" Johnny asked loudly.

"I'll handle it, John," said Crockett.

"We'll both handle it," his brother said. "I thought the loan was all set."

Howells looked ill, but suddenly his eyes changed. Quick footsteps sounded on the porch, and Gould walked in, Jason following right at his heels. Something in their manner warned Crockett. Gould, moving with a straight-backed confidence, frowned slightly as he came to a stop. The huge cowhand halted a foot behind him, eyeing Crockett like a troublesome dog.

"Let's go inside my office," Howells said, fingering his chin. "We can talk in there."

"Why?" asked Johnny.

"Your ranch," Howells said. "It concerns that."

"How does our spread concern Gould?"

"It's simple," Gould said. "I bought your land."

Johnny swore. The big cowhand took a step forward, the floor groaning under his weight, but a warning look from Gould held him back.

"We can go inside my office," Howells said. "I . . ."

Crockett's words silenced him. "I told you I was going to pay off the mortgage. How come you sold?"

"I . . . I explained that to you."

"Explain it again," Crockett said coldly.

"You had no money to pay. I had a good offer from Mr. Gould, and I took it."

"It's just simple business, Crockett," said Gould, his voice sure of itself. "You couldn't expect Howells to keep losing money on your ranch."

"We were going to pay up the mortgage," Johnny said, his narrow, unfriendly eyes glued to the stockman. "Ruel here was told he'd get the loan."

"There was nothing definite about a loan," Gould said quietly, but it didn't relieve the cold expression in his eyes. He glanced at Howells. "Did you promise a loan?"

"No. I only said I'd see what I could do."

Johnny looked at Crockett, his face confused. "You said there was a loan, Ruel?"

"Calm down, John," said Crockett. "This can be straightened out."

"You told me there was a loan," Johnny said, his face becoming hot and furious. "You let me go ahead and hire those hands on tick, thinkin' we had a loan."

"We rate a loan, John. And we'll get one. We won't lose the ranch like this. We . . ."

"Don't tell me anythin' about 'we'." Johnny swung away from his brother. Looking at Gould he added in the same dangerous voice, "I've got cattle now. And riders. I'm holdin' my ranch, you hear?"

Gould shook his head in disagreement. "It's my ranch," he said flatly. "I bought it, and my men will work it."

Johnny was suddenly calm, his voice quiet. "You don't send anyone onto my land," he said slowly. "I'll kill the first man who comes out." Then, he turned and started from the lobby.

Crockett took a few quick steps after him, grabbed his sleeve. "Johnny, wait. I'll . . ."

Johnny shook his arm free. "Don't say nothin', Ruel," he said in a hard voice. He continued on to the door and went outside.

Howells followed and shut the door behind Johnny. Hurriedly he pulled the green shade all the way down. Into the silence Crockett said, "Your business methods are rotten, Gould."

"I wouldn't cause any trouble if I were you," Gould answered. "You'd better go with your brother."

Crockett glanced at the shaded door. For an instant he stood perfectly still, his tall frame straight and tense. Then he turned and walked slowly back to Gould.

"I'm fighting that sale," he said softly. "You keep your men off Diamond C until it's settled."

"As far as I'm concerned it's all settled, Crockett. I'm having my riders start work there tomorrow, just as I'd planned."

"Then you'd better change your plans."

Gould glared at him. "You listen to me," he said. "If you look around this town, you'll see I don't change my plans. Hobart was nothing but a bunch of shacks when I came here. I built these five new buildings. And I'm building my home here." He hesitated, breathing deeply. "Now, get out."

The floorboards creaked slightly as Jason shifted his weight. One quick glance of Crockett's trained soldier's eyes imprinted the threat in his brain, the way the big fists clenched and unclenched, the wide stomach that suggested a flabbiness. This brute had had his way too long, and he was too sure of himself.

The knowledge was a weapon Crockett could use. He felt the jump of his pulse-beat, held down his cold fury.

"Keep your men off my land," he said, and deliberately turned so his right side faced Gould.

Gould looked at the giant. "Get him out of here, Jason," he said irritably. "Go ahead, throw him out."

The immense head bobbed up and down once in understanding, and, half-smiling with enjoyment, Jason stalked forward. He grabbed Crockett's shoulder, began to jerk him around.

Crockett whirled, bringing his elbow back violently into the middle of Jason's stomach. The force of the blow doubled the thick body over. Grunting, Jason straightened almost instantly and continued ahead in a more careful crouch.

Realizing he couldn't stand toe-to-toe and slug it out with this bulldog type of fighter, Crockett backed away to the right. He had to work fast or the brute's weight and mighty strength would wear him down. He stopped suddenly and feinted with his left to draw Jason in.

Jason took the bait. He surged forward, throwing his powerful right in a vicious roundhouse. Crockett side-stepped the blow by mere inches. The quick movement threw Jason off balance, giving Crockett the advantage he wanted.

He crowded the giant, smashing solid lefts and rights into the stomach. His third blow sunk in a little, the fourth went deeper. Jason cursed in surprised rage. He brought one immense arm down to cover his middle. The other arm swung out, reaching for a hold on Crockett.

Crockett jerked his body back. Grabbing air the huge cowhand floundered ahead clumsily. Crockett's right rose up, opened as it came down through a long arc, chopping like an axe against the thick neck. At the tremendous impact, Jason bellowed and straightened.

Instantly Crockett brought the right around again, the flat of his hand slashing into the big, reddened face, hitting the bridge of the nose. The bone snapped, flattened, gushed blood.

Jason screamed in pain, jerking his head back. Then, by sheer instinct, he lunged forward again. Crockett hit him three, four times in the stomach. The muscles there had no rigidity now. Jason staggered but did not fall.

Knowing he'd won, Crockett stayed in close and swung up from his waist. The uppercut smashed solidly into the throat just below the jawbone, landing with the crack of a hard-swung hickory singletree.

Jason spun around and dropped to the floor. He lay there choking as he fought to squeeze air into his lungs. He began to push himself up, but after a single try dropped flat again, using all his remaining strength to get his breath.

Crockett straightened, his chest rising and falling rapidly. He looked at Gould, saw how the stockman stared down at the prostrate giant. Howells' face was shocked. He edged back, away from Crockett.

"Remember what I said," Crockett told them. "You hold your cowhands off until we clear things up legally."

Gould's stare shifted to Crockett, saw the hard, narrowed eyes and tight mouth. Recognizing the danger to himself, he said, "I don't plan to do anything that's illegal."

"Just make sure you don't," Crockett said.

He kept his eyes on everyone as he moved toward the door. Then, he turned the knob and went outside.

Gould rubbed his smooth jaw and was silent for a full minute. Finally, he said, "Howells, you take the papers on Diamond C over to the marshal in the morning. I want the Crocketts off the ranch tomorrow."

"Tomorrow?" Unconsciously, Howells shot a glance at Jason, who was slowly climbing to his feet. He swallowed. "Crockett said he was going to fight it lega—"

"Legally?" Gould cut in. "Damn it, anything I do on my own land is legal. And those Crocketts'll be off there tomorrow, even if they have to be driven off."

Chapter Six

CROCKETT stepped down from the porch of the bank and crossed Pioneer with a long, deliberate stride. The satisfaction of the quick victory had rapidly faded, and just his stubborn, purposeful anger remained. He ignored the people who watched him. They could stare all they wanted, but they couldn't bother him now. His eyes were fastened only on Johnny's sorrel mare tied to the rail in front of Allison's general store.

He hastened his step as he went up onto the boardwalk. Ahead, Marion Howells appeared on the hotel porch. She was a handsome, stylish picture in the light brown dress of silk and lace she wore. From the intent way she watched his approach, he knew she had been waiting for him.

"You were at the bank," she asked him when he reached her. "Was there trouble?"

"Nothing happened to your brother," he said. "If that's what you mean."

Marion paid no attention to that. She glanced toward the bank. "You talked to Franklin Gould?"

"I did. We're not through talking though." He started to move past, but she laid a hand on his arm and he stopped.

"Mr. Crockett, I don't know what you're thinking," she said, "but don't try fighting Gould."

Her eyes held a strained look of concern. He watched her, thinking he'd never seen anything more lovely than her face, shadowed softly by the growing darkness.

His voice quieted. "I'm not planning to fight Gould," he said.

"You are. I can see it in your face." She gazed toward the bank again, nervously lifting her hand to smooth back a wisp of fine black hair stirred by the rising night breeze. When she spoke her voice was different, more comradely. "He has your ranch. Did he buy it legally?"

Crockett shrugged. "Legal is just a word to men like Gould—and your brother."

Her eyebrow lifted, but not in anger. "My brother has very little to say about any business he does with Franklin Gould. No one in Hobart has much to say when he wants something. You aren't the kind of man who can live like that. If I were you, I'd let my ranch go and leave here."

"No. You wouldn't leave here."

Marion stiffened, stared at him, but she did not answer.

"You stood up to Gould in the bank yesterday," he explained. "If you were really afraid of him, you'd leave your brother here to face him alone."

Slowly, she nodded. "William would be lost alone," she said. Her words sounded calm, but they were chosen very carefully. "But there's no need for a man like you..."

She paused, and Crockett waited, feeling suddenly close to this beautiful woman. In the silence he saw Johnny step out of Allison's store a block away and stop near the door to talk to someone inside. His glance returned to Marion Howells.

"A man like me can't just stand by while his home is stolen from him," he said.

Again she stiffened. "If you fight Gould, he'll use the army against you," she said urgently. "Don't do anything that will let him ruin you. Please."

"Gould won't ruin me," he said, touching the brim of his sombrero. Then, he continued on to the general store.

The prairie night was coming fast. Eastward the first faint stars winked in the darkened sky. An almost full moon hung above the horizon. Lantern light streamed from windows and doorways down onto Pioneer Street. Johnny's wide-shouldered silhouette turned away from the glaring brightness of the store doorway just before Crockett reached the porch.

Crockett stepped off the walk into the street. He reached the tie rail as Johnny began unhitching his sorrel mare. Johnny saw him but did not look up from what he was doing.

"What are you going to do, Johnny?" asked Crockett.

"Go back home. I've had enough of Gould, so ..."

"I'll come with you," Crockett said and noticed the frown growing on his brother's face. "I told Gould we'd fight this legally."

"There won't be anything legal about a carpetbagger court." Johnny looked tense, a mixture of anger and disappointment clear in his eyes. He climbed onto his horse, moving quickly and deliberately, like a man who'd made up his mind.

"Let me handle that," Crockett told him. "I can lick Gould on this in any court."

"Bein' a bluebelly ain't gonna help you none in this," Johnny retorted quickly. He began reining around.

Crockett felt the remark but knew it was only his brother's temper. He stepped in close to the horse and took hold of the bridle. "Johnny, we can do this without . . ."

"Let go," Johnny said.

"Johnny . . . ?"

Not answering, Johnny yanked his horse's head up, pulling it away. The sudden movement jerked the bridle free and snapped Crockett's sombrero from his head. Crockett knew better than to try to stop his brother now. He stood there motionless as Johnny swung the mare around and started down Pioneer at a lope.

Bending, Crockett lifted his hat from the dust.

"Just what are you going to do now?"

The sharp question came from behind and above him. Janet Bankhead stood on the porch, the light from the store behind her outlining the gentle curves and firm roundness that filled out her dress.

Worry lined her small face, but she was composed. For a moment they stared at each other in silence. Then she said, "Do you see what you've done to him?"

"What I've done to him?" Crockett said, looking at her coldly.

"I might have known," she said, watching him with something like wonder in her eyes. "You give him a hope and then see it torn away from him, but still you don't understand."

It jolted him. He was ready for anything but this. He knew she was bitter about the war, yet he thought she had at least understood that everything he'd done, everything he'd hoped, was as much for Johnny as himself.

"Nothing's been torn away from anyone," he said thickly. "Johnny and I will get Diamond C back."

Janet shook her small blonde head sadly. "If you believe that, you haven't learned much since you've come back. The law works only for the most powerful in Texas now. And the most powerful man here is Gould."

"And we should just quit. . . . Is that it?"

She smiled, but there was a touch of bitterness in her face. "You consider me an intruder. You feel I have no right to speak up in this, isn't that it?"

"I feel you have no right telling Johnny to quit," Crockett snapped. "He was all set to quit because of you when I got home. You had no right to do that."

"It's so easy for you," she said quickly, staring into the fury in his eyes. "But why can't you understand it isn't the same for Johnny?"

"I'll never understand why quitting is good for any man, Miss Bankhead."

"Do you believe meeting Gould with a gun is better? That's what Johnny wants to do."

He calmed, regretting that he'd spoken sharply to her. He saw now that there was more to her than just a pretty face and figure. Her defiance held a certain strength that would appeal to Johnny, a strength his brother needed.

"The problem isn't understanding Johnny," he said slowly. "It's keeping him from losing his temper until we can straighten everything out in court."

"And that's all you're going to do?"

"That and get our land back without having any gunplay."

She was silent, studying him like a worn-out store clerk being obviously civil to a customer she hoped would complete his business and leave. She said, "I think you'd better ride after him."

The weariness showing on her face told him there was nothing more he could say. He turned and started toward the livery stable.

Chapter Seven

IT WAS after eleven when the humped shapes of the oak grove and ranch buildings emerged shadowy and silent in the bright moonlight. In the pasture beyond the corral cattle were bedded down, ten or twelve vague shapes huddled against the ground. The cool night breeze stirring the leaves of the trees carried the wail of a coyote from the prairie far to the south. From somewhere in the grass edging the spring came the brittle chirp of a cricket.

The ranch house was dark. The long ride could have cooled Johnny's quick temper, Crockett felt; he might be asleep. Hashing out their problems would keep until morning. He slowed his mount and started quietly past the house.

He heard a sound to his left, at the corner of the house, and glanced that way. He could see three men standing there, silhouetted blackly against the lesser darkness of the night. His hand went back and down for his sixgun.

"That you, Ruel?" It was Johnny's voice, spoken just above a whisper.

"Yes."

Johnny's tall, broad-shouldered figure stepped forward. "You hear anyone on your back-trail?"

"No . . ." The others moved ahead hesitantly, halted and waited behind Johnny. Crockett could see their faces only faintly in the moonlight, but he knew it was Fauna and Little Joe Maddox. "What's going on, Johnny?" he asked.

"I figgered maybe Gould sent someone to follow you out."

"Gould? He won't do anything until tomorrow, John. He only got the ranch today."

"But he's already started pushin'," Johnny told him bitterly. "Brazos Helm jumped Fauna and Little Joe while they were drivin' the mavericks they branded back here. He took their iron."

"That's right," Little Joe Maddox added. "He said there was no more Diamond C, so we quit maverickin'."

Crockett said, "You quit just because he told you to?"

Little Joe's shadowed head and sombrero bobbed up and down in a nod. "You don't argue with an hombre like Brazos when he's holdin' a forty-four on you."

"Don't climb on these boys," Johnny said. "Nothin' they could do against Brazos."

Crockett was silent for a thoughtful minute. "Well, there's nothing we can do until morning. We might as well turn in and—"

"You turn in," Johnny said. "Brazos rode south after the Johnson boys. We're waitin' up in case they come ridin' in."

"You can wait inside as well as out here," Crockett said.

"We'll wait here," Johnny answered emphatically.

Mumbled words from Fauna and Little Joe echoed his decision. Crockett sat quietly for another few seconds, looking down at them, then nudged his claybank ahead.

Inside the barn, he took his time rubbing down King, then forked fresh hay into a bin. Johnny and the two cowhands were still standing in the yard when he went outside. They kept silent as he approached. Crockett walked into the house, trying to shrug off their attitude, but there was a measure of hurt within him. He'd felt these men had become a little closer to him out on the range today—but now this.

Then Crockett heard the clicking of boot heels on the porch. Johnny came in, carrying his Spencer. When he took off his sombrero, his blond hair was plastered damply against his head. His long arms were streaked with sweat and dust from the ride home.

Crockett asked, "Fauna and Little Joe leave?"

"They're out in the bunkhouse."

"There's room for them in there until Fred cleans..."

Johnny shook his head. "Fred's gone, Ruel. He ain't goin' to clean anythin' up." When he saw the questioning look on his brother's face, he added, "He must've left a long time 'fore Fauna and Little Joe got back tonight."

"You figure Brazos stopped here, too?"

"Someone did," Johnny said. He looked harassed and dejected. "I hope Gould keeps pushin', damn it." He laid the rifle down hard on the table, as though roughness somehow helped.

"There won't be any of that, John. What we do, we do through the law."

"Without any chance of winnin'? Them carpetbaggers'll ..."

"Let me worry about handling the carpetbaggers and Unionists," Crockett said. "My discharge from the Union Army will carry as much weight as Gould's word in this."

Johnny shook his head. "I don't want you usin' your discharge." A tone of sadness was mixed with his anger. "I hate havin' you even carryin' Union papers," he added, his voice rising. "I hated your fightin' for the North. You know that. I don't want any help from those papers. Can't you understand that?"

"You should be glad I've got them," Crockett offered. "They're the only thing that'll get our ranch back."

"Glad ... glad my own brother's a turncoat Texan?" Johnny said slowly. "That'd be a laugh if I didn't feel it so much, Ruel. Look, I always thought you were quite a man. Next to Pa, you were my idol as a kid. I used to be satisfied just to go ridin' with you. I sat on that pole fence out there watchin' you every time you broke a horse. It was the biggest thing in my life to be close to you."

"You're my kid brother, Johnny. If I were the younger, it would've been the same with me as it was with you."

Johnny didn't seem to hear. "Then you had that shootout with Tom Allison," he went on. "I got this Spencer out and stayed down in the grove all that afternoon, waitin' in case Tom's brothers came after you." Hesitating for a moment, he rested both hands palm-down on the table, leaning forward toward his brother. "After you rode North, I went into town and walked the streets, darin' people to say somethin' against you to me. I'd've killed them if they had."

Crockett said slowly, "And my discharge papers changed that?"

"Changed it?" Johnny echoed in a soft, definite voice. "I stayed home with Pa, Ruel. I watched him go dirt poor because the markets and ports of the South were closed. I watched him take all the hate the neighbors built up for him because of you."

"Pa could stand that, Johnny. He came out here because he believed in something. He let me have my beliefs, too."

"Well, I couldn't take it," Johnny said bitterly. "You know what I did? I joined the Confederate Army. I told myself it was to make up for you being with the Union. But the real reason was because I couldn't stand around and watch everythin' it was doin' to Pa."

Silence fell between them, and in the drawn-out quiet the brothers stared at each other Shortly, Crockett said, "You should have told me this when I got home, Johnny. You can't keep holding hate inside."

"I don't hate you, Ruel."

"Then what would you call it?"

"Ruel, I was glad when you came back. When we decided to build up again, I hoped we could help everyone else around here get on their feet. I hoped they'd forget about you fightin' for the North." He straightened suddenly, pounding his fist on the table. "Now Gould's tryin' to ruin that. Well, I won't let him do it to us."

"Calm down," Crockett said, drawing a deep breath. "Just don't try using that gun for a while. Let me take it to court first. Pa had over a thousand head when the war started, so we still rate mavericking while we're fighting Gould."

Johnny said flatly, "Gould only understands force. That's all I want to try."

"Try my way first, Johnny." Crockett paused, then said in a serious, even voice, "If it doesn't work, I'll go along with what you want."

"You'd fight Gould?"

"If it's the only way left, yes."

For a minute Johnny looked at him in thoughtful silence. Finally he said, "All right, Ruel. I'll try it your way. And we'll see."

Sleep did not come easily to Crockett. The realization of the sorrow his actions had caused his father and Johnny brought a new weight of obligation over him.

For a long time he lay, thinking. Then weariness crept over him and he slept.

Chapter Eight

IT SEEMED he had hardly slept at all when he was awakened at daylight by the rapid drum of running hoofbeats. Climbing down to the floor he saw that Johnny was already up. He crossed to the door and looked out. The Johnson brothers were coming into the yard from the south. Judging from the white dripping from the horses' bits, they'd been run hard and heavily a good long time.

Johnny had come out of the barn, followed by Fauna and Little Joe. The riders headed for where they stood, straightening back in their stirrups as they reined in.

Scrap Johnson, a tall, thin man in a black shirt, swung down immediately and began talking excitedly to Johnny. His brother Al stayed in the saddle, keeping his horse beside the grouped men. He picked up the talk from Scrap and was waving one hand wildly toward the flat and speaking fast when Crockett got near enough to hear what he was saying.

"Took our runnin' iron, I tell you," he called loudly, as if the listeners were a long way off. "He took it and told us t' git."

Crockett asked, "Brazos again?"

"Yes," Johnny said, turning to face him. "Al says he headed south when he rode off."

Nodding, Crockett was thoughtful. The cowhands watched him, quiet and angry-looking. Then Little Joe muttered into the silence, "There's six of us. We can take Brazos if we go after him together."

"No," Crockett told him emphatically. "If we go into that rough country after him, we'd be sitting ducks."

"What do we do," asked Little Joe. "Sit on our tails 'til he comes after us one at a time?"

Crockett said, "We work in teams out in the open,

48

so there'll be no chance of Brazos jumping anyone. If he is foolish enough to try it, there'll be plenty of time to give him a good welcome."

He paused, but none of the others spoke.

He gestured toward the flat where the twelve head of Diamond C cattle were grazing in the warm morning sun. "We'll brand every maverick we can find in the open and gather them into that herd Fauna and Little Joe started. We—"

"Hey, look there!" Al Johnson's sudden yell cut in. He'd turned in the saddle to point to the northeast. Because of his height he'd been first to notice the small cloud of dust far out on the flat. Now the others could see it.

Leaning forward, Al reached into his brother's saddlebag and took out a pair of Confederate Army binoculars. He raised them to his eyes and said, "That's banker Howells' surrey . . . and Bol Taylor's there, too."

Johnny took the glasses. All were quiet while he looked. "Gould, Jason and two more," he said slowly. "Bud Kincaid and Rube Canby, I think."

The last two named were Gould's hired hands. Movement and muttering began among the watchers. The heated small talk, punctuated by an occasional curse, kept up while the riders approached. Frowning, Crockett kept his eyes on Johnny, sensing the tension that gripped his brother.

"Remember," Crockett said quietly. "No trouble."

Johnny nodded. "I said you'd get your try."

Still frowning, Crockett stepped forward from the others. Howells' surrey was clear to him, an expensive eastern-built vehicle drawn by a pair of matched bays. A single glance of Crockett's stockman's eye judged the dark gray stallion Gould rode as one of the finest bred horses he'd ever seen. The wide bandage on Jason's nose stood out white in the glaring sunlight. The immense cowhand squatted in the saddle, his huge shoulders sagged forward by the weight of his arms. Tense hate was clear in his large black eyes, but Crockett gave him no notice. He looked only at the marshal, who pulled out into the lead once he reached the yard.

Bol Taylor raised his right hand in a friendly gesture as he reined in. "Howdy, boys." His gaze went to Crockett while he dismounted. "Long ride out here, Ruel."

"What'll you have, Bol?"

"You know," the tall mustached lawman said gently but firmly. "Mr. Gould owns this spread now."

"I'm taking the sale into court. Didn't Gould tell you that?"

"Court or no court, he has the mortgage, Ruel. And he doesn't want anyone on this land."

The other riders had reached the spot where the marshal had left his horse. Gould dismounted and passed the reins of his stallion to Jason. The other two cowhands hung back, but, as Gould came forward, Howells climbed down from the seat of the surrey and followed him. The banker took some papers from his pocket, held them as he would a weapon.

Gould stopped beside Bol Taylor. "Well, what are you waiting for, Marshal?"

"You boys get your belongings," said the marshal. "You'll be given time to take everything that's yours."

Crockett spoke up. "We're not leaving here until we settle it in court, Bol."

Taylor straightened, stood stiff-legged. "Look," he said, his mustached face getting hard, "I'm just doing my job here The law says Mr. Gould owns this land. As long as he holds the mortgage, I'll enforce it."

Howells held out the papers he'd brought along. "Everything is here," he announced. Crockett's eyes met his, and he added weakly, "If you want to look at them."

"Save those papers for court," Crockett said.

"There's been enough of this talk," said Gould. "This land is private property now, bought and paid for and registered. You get off now, or there'll be trouble. Is that clear enough for you?" He glanced sideways at the marshal, as if reminding him of his duty.

Taylor's eyes sparkled with anger. "All right, boys. I'm telling you for the last time to get going."

Silence fell, a taut, heavy silence. Gould looked back

at the mounted cowhands. "You move your rolls into the house and . . ." he began.

"Don't try it, Gould," Johnny said evenly.

Gould's smooth face stared at him for a moment, and a small cynical smile lined the corners of his mouth. He spoke to the riders again. "After you drop your rolls, go haze that cattle in closer to the building over there."

Johnny took a step forward. "That's our cattle. Don't go near them." The tone of his voice made the cowhands hesitate.

Crockett moved next to his brother. "John, take it easy," he said softly, as if soothing a skittish horse. He heard Gould say, "Damn you men, didn't I tell you to get started?"

The riders began moving their mounts.

"Stay here!" Johnny yelled.

But the cowhands kept going. Johnny's hand went down, came up with his .44 cocked and aimed.

"Stop right there!" he ordered. His face was red with rage.

Instantly the riders jerked their horses to a halt. Gould's face showed surprise, but he did not let the gun hold him back. He glanced at the marshal. "You're the law. Get that gun away from him."

"All right, Johnny," Bol Taylor said, taking a step ahead. "Put it away."

Crockett said quietly, "Put it back, John." If it was handled right there'd be no shooting, but it had to be handled calmly.

"I won't put it away," Johnny said, edging back from the marshal. "Ain't bad enough that buzzard's got our ranch. Now he wants our cattle."

"Everything here belongs to me," Gould said. "Marshal?"

Bol Taylor was closer to Johnny now. "That gun's raised against the law," he said quietly. "Now, you give it here and we'll forget this happened."

His arm shot out and, grabbing Johnny's hand, wrenched at the gun to pull it free. Johnny's arm jerked up to break the lawman's grip.

"Don't! Don't, Marshal!" Crockett yelled, stepping

in to separate them, but the gun exploded, the blast
drowning out his words.

Crockett saw the wild bullet strike Howells' shoulder,
heard the banker's shocked scream. The impact of the
bullet whirled the banker around and threw him backwards off the heels of his patent-leather shoes and under the hoofs of Gould's stallion. Crockett dove for
the fallen man and pulled him clear of the threat of a
trampling.

Johnny still held the six-gun level. "Get back!" he
said. The silver barrel was centered on Gould's stomach.
"Get out of here!"

Marshal Taylor stepped back. His hand was well
clear of his holster. "Mr. Gould's unarmed!" he said.
"Don't shoot, boy!"

"Get off my land," Johnny said. What he'd done had
begun to register, and there was a slight tremble to his
hand. "Get off!"

"We're going." Gould stared directly into Johnny's
face, spoke slowly, then began backing toward his stallion.

"Here, give me a hand," Crockett said to the stockman. He had Howells' coat and shirt open and was
feeling for the vein that fed the wound. The blood was
warm and slippery to his fingers.

Gould bent down. He held the shirt open while Crockett worked. Howells was mumbling incoherently, groaning. Bol Taylor joined them and saw that the bleeding
was almost stopped.

"Went all the way through high up . . . missed the
bone, I think," Crockett said to the lawman. "You better get him back to Doc Ford."

Taylor nodded. He straightened and walked to
the surrey, very much aware of Johnny holding the
Colt and the quietly watching, motionless cowhands.
He led the matched bays back until the vehicle was
even with Howells. Johnny still held the gun ready,
but it was clear he was worried.

Crockett had made a tourniquet with his bandanna,
and, after it was tied, Gould helped him lift the wounded man into the surrey. Taylor quickly clambered up
onto the seat.

Howells' body trembled and he groaned as they moved him. Then he fainted.

"Easy . . . easy, now," Crockett said. Turning to the mounted cowhands, he snapped, "One of you get up in the seat and keep hold of him. What's the matter with you?"

Jason dismounted and climbed up beside the marshal. Crockett held Howells still until the cowhand had a firm grasp on him. His eyes met the marshal's, and he said, "Get him back fast, Bol."

Taylor nodded. He shot one glance at Johnny. "Come in now," he said. "It'll be easier on you."

"No. You won't take me in."

"We'll come after you. You know . . ."

Gould's hard voice cut in. "Don't waste time on him, Taylor. Let's get going." He kept watching Johnny as he mounted, an ugly look in his eyes.

Taylor waited until Gould had turned his stallion. Then, he gave the reins a slight shake and the surrey moved forward slowly, turned in a wide circle and left the yard.

Johnny holstered the Colt, silently watching the surrey and riders skirt the oak grove and go onto the flat.

"That wasn't your fault," Little Joe Maddox said. "Bol made you shoot. I'll testify to that."

"I saw it, too," Al Johnson stammered. "I—I saw how he hit your arm. That made the gun fire . . ."

"Yeah. Bol made you shoot," Little Joe repeated. He looked around him, his eyes going from face to face. "Y'all saw it. Y'all will testify?"

"Sure," Scrap Johnson agreed. He kept nodding his head while the others let out a stream of yesses.

Crockett watched Johnny. He'd caught Gould's final glance, too, and he knew the stockman would push this all the way. He said, "You'd do right to go in now, Johnny. They . . ."

"And face a carpetbagger judge?" Johnny shook his head. Then, suddenly, he turned and walked toward the house.

Little Joe called after him, "Hey, we'll be witnesses for you." He started to follow Johnny but stopped when Crockett said, "I'll talk to him. Saddle our horses, will you?"

Crockett went into the house. Johnny was standing at the table. He had already taken some beans from the cabinet, and now he was making up his war bag.

"What are you going to do?" Crockett asked him.

Johnny looked up. "What do you think I'm doin'? Nothin' I can do but run."

"You start running, Johnny, you'll never do anything but run the rest of your life."

Johnny stared at him, breathing heavily. He said, "If I go back, the least I'll get is time. I'm not spendin' half my life in some Yankee jail. And if Howells dies, they'll hang me."

"That bullet went clean through," Crockett told him. "He won't die. It isn't worth ruining your life for a man like him."

"It isn't worth dyin' for, either." Crouching, Johnny pulled a box from beneath his bunk. When he stood, he held two small bags containing round balls and fine rifle powder for his muzzle-loading Colt. Carefully, he added them to the rest of his belongings.

"Listen to me for a minute," Crockett said, drawing in a deep breath, frightened a little by the calm, sure way Johnny was going about this. "You've got seven witnesses. The jury will have to be local men. There's no way they can be too hard on you. You . . ."

"Drop it," Johnny said flatly. "Nothin'll change my mind. I'm waitin' 'round 'til tonight. And after I see Janet I'm ridin'."

"Janet?" Crockett asked quickly. Something was coming into his mind that told him he hadn't failed.

"She'll understand about this," Johnny said. He hesitated, then added in an even, thoughtful voice, "She'll go along in this with me."

"You're going to ask her to run, too?"

"She can meet me some place."

"You're dumber than I thought," Crockett said angrily. He knew he was taking a step he could never retrace, but it was his only chance. "Running yourself is one thing, but asking her to run is downright stupid."

Johnny straightened, stared hard at his brother.

"We'll make our own decisions, Ruel. We'll do what we think is right."

"Then take her with you. Ask her to hole up with you until the army catches up. Ask her to die with you."

For a full minute Johnny stood there staring, swallowing hard. Finally, he said, "I'm going, Ruel. But I've got to see Janet first." He lifted the food and war bag and started for the door.

Crockett grabbed his arm. "Johnny, don't lose everything..."

"Let go," Johnny said, jerking his arm free.

Crockett remained motionless. He couldn't watch his brother throw away his life because he himself had failed in this. He strode out the door and went quickly down the steps to where the cowhands stood with his and Johnny's horses.

Johnny was climbing into the saddle amid a lot of confused talk. Crockett hesitated beside King, checking the cinch out of habit. As he mounted, Johnny turned his sorrel mare and started from the yard, heading south.

"You men go back to town," Crockett told the cowhands. Then he rode after his brother.

The fierce rays of the morning sun pouring down from the cloudless blue sky had even this early reheated the prairie grassland to blast furnace intensity. Johnny kept his mount at a slow lope, and Crockett caught up right away. When he pulled his gelding in alongside, Johnny glanced around, already the fugitive checking his back-trail.

"No reason for you to run, too, Ruel," he said flatly.

Crockett looked into the gray eyes, saw how they were dulled with weariness. "Janet's the other way, Johnny," he said.

"I figure to run south awhile and cut back to Humphrey's old spread. That'll give Taylor and the Army something to follow. Give me the time I need."

Nodding, Crockett did not answer. He did little talking during the next hour and a half, but when he did speak he made certain Janet Bankhead came into the talk in some way. Johnny became more thoughtful, hardly spoke at all after they swung east across the prairie toward the deserted Humphrey ranch buildings.

Carl Humphrey had been one of the smaller cattlemen in the county before he sold out to Franklin Gould and went west into New Mexico. His main house was just a single-roomed adobe building. Crockett and Johnny circled around so they came in behind the pole corral to the left of the barn. They took the horses inside the house with them, got hay from the barn and settled down to wait.

The soldiers they knew would come passed late that afternoon, a column of six blue-clad cavalrymen moving along at a canter. Even at a distance of two miles they could tell the lone civilian in the detail was Bol Taylor. The pack horse led by the soldier bringing up the rear was evidence enough that they expected to be out a good long time.

Johnny sat by the glassless window, silent until the column disappeared from view behind a mesquite thicket to the southwest. Finally he stood, looking thoughtful.

"You really think there's a chance of getting out of this, Ruel?" he asked quietly.

"If it's done right, there is."

His brother remained silent.

"Howells will have the most say in court," Crockett said. "If I can get to him and make an agreement, we ..."

"What kind of an agreement?"

"The ranch, John. Howells knows I'll eventually win in court because I'm a Union veteran. If I agree to let Diamond C go, it'll help him with Gould."

"With Bol Taylor out of town, I'd get shot as soon as I rode in. One of Gould's men'd—"

"I'll have Howells notify the Army. One word from him and you'll get an escort."

There was a wetness in Johnny's eyes and his blond-stubbled face was twisted with feeling. "Try it, Ruel," he said. "Try it."

Just before nine that night they reached Hackberry Creek. They left the flat, illuminated brightly in the floodlight glare of the moon, two miles south of Hobart.

Staying in the cover of the timber, they followed the stream north to a grassy hollow a quarter-mile below the Army encampment. The surrounding moss-covered oaks and brush offered ample covering for Johnny until Crockett could finish his business. From here Johnny could watch the prairie to the west and the wagon road to the east. There was little chance of his being surprised.

"If Howells is willing," Crockett reminded his brother, "I'll ride back here. If not, I'll keep on the road and meet you back at Humphrey's."

In the moonlight filtering through the trees, he saw Johnny's nod. "Tell Janet, Ruel."

"No, not even Janet. Until you're safe in jail, no one knows you're here."

Johnny nodded silently. Crockett kneed his gelding ahead and, after another hundred yards, cut onto the worn wagon road.

Chapter Nine

BRAZOS HELM turned off Pioneer Street and made his way down the length of the alleyway to the back of the building that housed Gould's office. He stopped in the deep shadows and knocked at the door. Inside, muffled footsteps sounded, and then Gould's voice said, "Who is it?"

"Brazos."

A key clicked in the lock, and the door swung back. Blinking from the sudden bright lamplight, Brazos stepped inside.

"I thought you'd have him with you," Gould said.

"Damned if I can find him," said Brazos. "I looked in every saloon in town. At the hotel, too." He halted at the heavy mahogany desk and leaned against the top. "You sure Limpy's in town?"

"Of course I'm sure. Jason saw him at the livery stable when we got back this morning."

"I don't know. I think you're goin' at this all wrong, Gould." Brazos had taken tobacco and paper from his shirt pocket, and he bent his head low while he made a smoke.

Gould felt sudden anger at the man's calling him by his last name. But he curbed it and said smoothly, "You would've killed Limpy right away?"

"That's right."

"And everything would have been stopped then and there," Gould said, his words low and cold. "Those Army men aren't fools, you know. They would have looked further with both of them dead."

Brazos inserted the cigarette between his lips. He looked at Gould as he lighted it. "Well, I could go after the Crocketts. Any time you say, I'm willin'."

"I realize that. And it might come with Ruel Crockett."

"Only him?"

"Yes. I'm sure Taylor and the Army will take care of Johnny. Once they corner him, there'll be only one way to finish it. But if Crockett stays around yelling for a trial, I'll have to count on you."

"You just say the word, Gould," Brazos said, and he exhaled a mouthful of smoke. "And have the money ready."

At the repeated use of his name, Gould's shoulders stiffened. He watched Brazos, seeing how he eyed the book-filled shelves that ran along two of the office walls. He had contempt for what he saw in the gunman, but Brazos was as necessary now as the money he used in his business. In a way he was more useful. More money could always be secured, but he'd never get a substitute for a fast gun like Brazos.

"You read all them books, Gould?"

"Most of them. But I don't have much chance for reading now."

Brazos smiled. "I always wanted to own books with leather covers. I . . ."

He straightened, his hand dropping by instinct as a quick knocking pounded on the door. Gould turned. Both men heard Jason's deep voice. "Open up . . . hey, open up."

Gould unlocked the door. Jason entered half-carrying Fred Hardin. His immense arm was clamped around the old man's bony shoulders in a bear-hug that could immediately put an end to any struggling.

Jason dropped his burden in a mahogany chair beside the desk. Hardin sat doubled over, one hand rubbing at his shoulder. The smell of raw liquor reeked around him.

"He was up in Sutton's loft," Jason told Gould. "I think he was tryin' to hide from us."

"Is that right?" Gould asked the white-haired old man. "Why should you feel you've got to hide from us, Fred?"

Hardin straightened stiffly, but kept his eyes on the floor.

"Come on, Fred," said Gould again. "Why should you feel you have to hide from us?"

He went behind the desk and sat, casually, as though he were simply having a friendly conversation. He leaned forward, letting his long arms rest on the blotter. "Do you think you have to be afraid of us, Fred?"

Hardin's eyes flicked about the room, sliding past Jason and Brazos. He shook his head slowly.

"I was sleepin' one off. I wasn't hidin'," he said.

Gould nodded. "You were out at Diamond C with the Crocketts. Did you do much talking with them?"

"No, not about . . . I didn't talk with them at all."

"Not about anything?" Gould's words were quiet but insistent.

Again the bony, white-haired head shook. "The only thing they said to me was they was payin' off the mortgage. That's all."

Gould's eyebrow went up. He looked as if he was enjoying this. "Did you hear about what happened out there today? About Howells?"

"Yes," Hardin said, hesitated to swallow hard. "I heard. I heard 'bout the shootin'. And 'bout the reward for Johnny."

"The reward," Gould said smiling. "Two thousand would be a big fortune to anyone who brought him in. Any man could use that kind of money."

"That's a lot of money," Hardin said.

"That reminds me." Gould leaned back in his chair. "You still have your job on the ranch if you want it." He opened a side drawer and took out a roll of bills. He counted the dollars casually, then laid the money near Hardin's hand. "Your first month's pay. Take it, Fred."

Hardin stared at the money, but made no move to pick it up.

"Go ahead, Fred. It's no crime for a man to take money from his employer. Take it."

"I'm not good for much ranch work," Hardin said. "My leg—"

"You're capable of doing what I want," interrupted Gould. He pushed the money closer with his fingertips. As Hardin picked up the bills, Gould added, "You work for me now. I expect loyalty first from all my employees. I want you to remember that, Fred."

The white-haired old man nodded. Gould stood, looked at Jason. "Why don't you take Fred down to the Casino for a few drinks?"

"Sure . . . sure, Mr. Gould," said Jason. He put one big hand around Hardin's arm, and he walked with the limping little man to the door.

When they were gone, Brazos rose from his seat and stretched. "Mebbe it's all the books you read," he said.

"Books?" said Gould.

"Yeah. The way you handled that. Mebbe you picked it up in some book."

"It worked," Gould said confidently. "That talk I had with him last year. And this one."

Brazos considered the words, grinned. "And there I was thinkin' them rides I took out to Diamond C had somethin' to do with keepin' Limpy shut."

The thumping of heavy footsteps outside in the alleyway made them both look towards the door. The knob turned, and Jason, his wide face flushed, ran in. In his haste, his boot heel caught on the threshold and he almost stumbled.

"Mr. Gould," he said breathing heavily. "Crockett's in town. I jest seen him goin' into the hotel."

"The hotel? You sure?"

"Yuh . . . ," Jason answered. "An' he's wearin' his gun. I figger he might be gonna see—"

"All right! Shut up! I'm not stupid!"

Gould opened the desk's middle drawer, took out a stubby double-barreled Remington derringer and put it into his pocket. That brought instant silence. Then he closed the desk and locked it. When he came out from behind, Brazos spoke up.

"You say the word, Gould, and Crockett won't get out of Howells' room."

"No. That would be stupid right now."

Brazos Helm's face hardened. "Mebbe you should be careful who you call stupid, Gould." He dropped his cigarette onto the floor and ground it out with his boot heel.

Gould's voice froze. "You won't bother Crockett. Not yet, do you hear?"

The gunfighter reflected on this, scowling. "Sure," he said. "You pay the bills. But I think I'll jest take me a walk 'round town while you're inside. I need the air, Gould."

In the hotel hallway Crockett knocked on Howells' door and waited. Coming into town he'd seen the posters offering a two thousand dollar reward for his brother, and that worried him. There'd be more danger to Johnny now, from the type of men who'd be attracted by all that money.

He heard muted footsteps inside. Then the door opened. A small dark-skinned Mexican woman looked out. "Señor?" she said.

"I'd like to talk to Mr. Howells."

The woman shook her head. "Señor Howells is very sick . . ." she began, but a door opening behind her made her stop. She looked around as Marion Howells entered the parlor.

Seeing Crockett, Marion said, "It's all right, Anna." She was wearing what on any other woman would be a simple white cotton dress; on her, with the top buttons opened for coolness, it gave startling emphasis to her dark beauty. She came toward him, a frown gathering on her smooth forehead.

The Mexican servant was going into a side room. Crockett motioned toward her. "She told me your brother is very bad," he said.

"He had a fever, but the doctor said he'll be all right. He's sleeping now."

Crockett nodded. "We're sorry about the shooting. It was a mistake, Marion."

"William told me," she said. Stopping beside him, she put her hand on his arm, and he could feel the tension in her. "You shouldn't have come here. There are reward posters up all over Hobart."

"The reward's for Johnny. Not for me."

"But Franklin Gould is spreading talk that you'd run with Johnny. He sent the marshal out to hunt you both down."

She moved closer to him, eyes wide and troubled. He was aware of the touch of her dress, could smell the faint hint of her perfume. Suddenly, he was immensely gladdened by her concern, drawn to her by it.

"If I could talk to your brother, there won't be any-one being hunted down," he said. Quickly, he went on and told her about Johnny's willingness to give him-self up.

"He's waiting out there now?" she said.

"Yes. There's too much danger coming in without—"

"Marion?" Howells' low voice came from the bed-room, interrupting him. "Marion?"

She glanced around, looked thoughtfully at the bed-room door. "I don't know . . ." she began. Then, the tension went out of her hand, and she let go of Crock-ett's arm. "Please don't take long," she said.

Turning, she started across the parlor. He followed, noticing how gracefully she moved. Once again he felt a definite closeness to this woman. Watching her now, thinking how nice she'd been every time they'd met was a natural thing. He found it pleasurable, but he quickly stopped his thoughts from dwelling on her.

Her parlor, with its thick rugs and fine furnishings, was an abrupt change from the things Crockett knew. Everything here, her stylish and expensive clothing and her mode of living, was as out of place in this Texas frontier town as Crockett had been in New York and Washington. It was all right for a while, but then a person had to return to the life he'd always known. With Marion it would be the same. Once her brother's business was finished here, she'd happily return to her own fashionable world back East.

Marion opened the bedroom door and entered first. She went directly to the small table at the head of her brother's bed and busied herself pouring a glass of water.

Howells was propped up on two pillows. His face seemed as white as the large bandage covering his shoulder. He nodded weakly when Crockett halted beside the bed. With his good hand he pushed back the wisps of hair hanging down over his brow.

"I heard you tell Marion your brother wants to give himself up," he said.

"Yes. We were hoping it would go easier for Johnny if I talked it over with you first."

Howells took the glass his sister held out to him. He sipped as he studied Crockett. Finally he said, "You're offering some kind of a deal."

"If you want to call it that," Crockett answered. "My brother's life could be at stake in this. I'd let Diamond C go if it would help him."

He knew Marion was staring, but he gave her no notice. He waited while Howells sipped the water again. The quiet of the room was broken only by a rapping sound coming in from the parlor. When Howells looked up again, he was smiling.

"I'd like all the trouble over your ranch straightened out," he said. "I know I can . . ." He hesitated, stiffened as his gaze went to the doorway behind Crockett.

Crockett turned to see Franklin Gould walking in. The stockman was frowning slightly. He stopped at the end of the bed, his eyes flickering from face to face.

"What's going on here?" he asked bluntly.

Howells said, "Mr. Crockett came in about his brother."

"The law will take care of his brother. You know that."

"They're willing to drop all claim to Diamond C," Howells said a bit proudly, "if I agree to go easy on . . ."

"There's no reason for you to go easy on a man who shot you," Gould said.

The banker half-smiled. "I said the Crocketts are willing to drop all claim to Diamond C," he explained again.

"How long since a hunted man has any claim to anything?" Gould said coldly, his hard eyes warning Howells.

Howells did not answer. He simply stared down into the glass he held. Crockett noticed how tense Marion had suddenly become—and that verified his own vague fear. He watched the banker, feeling the rising chill of disappointment. But he had to make a final try. He spoke once again.

"It's up to you, Mr. Howells." he said.

Gould said, "There'll be no deals." He seemed to have relaxed, but it didn't change the hard expression about his eyes as he added to Howells, "That's what you were going to say?"

"Yes," Howells said. "That's what I was going to say."

Now Gould smiled faintly. "I'd say the only thing for you and your brother to do is clear out of Texas." His mouth stayed open to add to that, but the sudden outbreak of gunfire somewhere below in the street made him turn.

Marion stepped back to the window and raised the shade. For a minute she was quiet, pressing against the glass to see.

Finally, she said, "It was near the general store . . ."

Crockett moved to her side fast. He pulled back the curtain, saw the people running through the lamplit street. It looked to him as if a small crowd was already gathering in the alleyway between Allison's store and the barber shop. Those in the rear were standing on tip-toe, trying to see something at the back end of the alley.

A sudden cold fear began growing in him. He swung around, started to leave. Marion caught his arm. Her mouth trembled in the glare of the wall lamp.

"Your brother was waiting for you," she said. "You don't think . . ."

"I don't know," he said. Then he went from the bedroom.

Outside, the street was how he knew it would be after a shooting: lights on all over the place, some of the people in the excited crowd carrying lanterns so they could see better. He passed two women in a doorway, standing there talking in whispers. Children bounded back and forth behind the crowd, making attempts to peer past the grown-ups. One boy had climbed onto another's shoulders, and already the one on the bottom was calling for his turn to look.

Crockett shoved his way through the crowd, his elbows jabbing and raking anyone in his path. At the rear of the alleyway he broke out of the buildings' dark shadows and into the small moonlit yard behind the general store.

Six or seven men, one of them holding a lantern, were bent over a body lying under an old cottonwood. The closest man was Allison. The elderly storekeeper glanced around and saw Crockett.

For a moment Allison stared, his mouth opened slightly. Then he started back to meet Crockett.

"Ruel," he said, "I'd've gotten you if I had known where you were."

Crockett felt the cold fear become icy. "Johnny?" he said, anticipating the answer.

The storekeeper's gray head nodded. "He came in to talk to Janet," he said, his voice almost a whisper. "It was in the back, Ruel. He never had a chance."

Chapter Ten

CROCKETT stood motionless, looking beyond Allison to the men gathered around his brother's body. "Dead," he said, his voice soft in the quiet night. "I was hoping— How did it happen?"

"Johnny came in by the back door. He talked to Janet for a few moments. When he left someone shot him."

"Janet saw it?"

"She was with Johnny when he left the store. But I don't think she saw the killer." He glanced around toward the building. "She's inside, Ruel. She's taking it hard."

Crockett nodded slowly. He walked to where his brother lay, a hard, frozen expression on his face. The man holding the lantern recognized him and straightened. He stepped aside quickly, clearing the way. He watched Crockett solemnly, awkwardly.

"I'm sorry," he said. "Sure sorry." And, as if an afterthought, "We'll move him soon as Doc comes."

Nodding, Crockett stared at his brother's body, his features deliberate, thoughtful. Johnny lay face down in the sand. Two wide bloodstains made the back of his shirt look black in the colorless moonlight filtering through the cottonwood leaves. His head was hatless, his face still twisted with shocked surprise and pain. He couldn't wait to see his girl, Crockett thought. Why? Why couldn't he have waited?

Hunkering down beside the quiet pained face, he brushed the dirt from Johnny's forehead. A tremor of emotion ran through his body, bringing with it a pain that pressed against his chest like a crushing weight.

The shuffle of many footsteps came from behind him, and he became aware of the low talk of the watching crowd. An old Mexican close by crossed himself, mumbled a prayer. Another man muttered, "In the back, damn it. . . . Damn it!" Others picked that up, echoed the feeling.

Unconsciously, Crockett brushed lightly once more at the dust on the still forehead. Then he stood. The man beside him said, "We'll git who did it, don't you worry. We'll git him."

Crockett caught the reflection of lamplight from a star on the speaker's wide chest. Looking directly at the man, he saw it wasn't Bol Taylor, but Al Cox, a taller, younger lawman in a wide-brimmed, high-crowned stiff sombrero.

"What for, deputy?" Crockett asked. "To give him his reward?"

"Johnny was my friend," the deputy said. His eyes were tight as he stared back.

Swallowing hard, Crockett nodded. "I know, Al," he said quietly. "I know." Without looking at the young lawman he turned slowly and strode toward the back door of the general store.

The crowd opened up for him, those in close avoiding his eyes. As he passed, the onlookers doing most of the talking quieted but resumed their conversations once they believed he was beyond earshot. Already some of the people lining the rear of the crowd had seen enough of the tragedy and, singly or in groups, were breaking away and starting back along the alley.

Crockett opened the door and went through the small room Allison used for storage. Janet was standing just inside the main store. The redness around her eyes told him she had been crying, but now she seemed calm and composed.

For a few seconds they looked at each other in silence. Then he said, "Mr. Allison told me you saw what happened."

Janet shook her head. "I didn't see the shooting," she said, trying to control the shakiness in her voice. "I'd closed the door behind Johnny before the shooting began."

"You didn't see anything? What did you do, hear the shots and not even bother looking outside?"

She stared at him, her small face becoming ghastly pale in the light of the overhanging lamp. "I looked out," she whispered. "Yes, I went out." Her composure broke. She turned her face away from him, began to cry.

He went closer to her and put a hand on her arm. "Janet . . ." he began.

"Don't touch me!" she cried suddenly, jerking away from him. "This is all your fault . . . don't touch me!"

"My fault?" His voice was low and thick.

"You and your big plans." She looked around at him, her wet eyes filled with pain and fury. "You took over everything when you came back. You made Johnny go along with your plans. Everything you wanted to do, he did. Well, look out there! Look out in the yard! That's where all your big plans got him!"

She gave way completely then and stood there, weeping uncontrollably. He took her thin shoulders in his hands and turned her so she'd have to face him. When she tried to glance away again, he tightened his grip, forcing her to look at him.

"I don't want any wasted talk," he said bitterly. "I don't expect you to understand what I was trying to do." His voice became sharper, tighter. "But you're the only one who could've seen the man who killed my brother. Now, you tell me what happened when you went outside."

She kept crying for another minute. When she stopped, she ran the back of her hand across her lips. "It was too dark," she said. "I couldn't see anything. I almost tripped over . . . I didn't even see Johnny lying there in the dark at first."

"You didn't see anyone. Or hear anything?"

"I only heard someone running away. I heard that." She stopped, her breath coming slowly. "By the time I got to Johnny I couldn't hear it any more. People started shouting. Mr. Allison came out of the store. I couldn't even tell in which direction the running was going."

"Can you remember anything else? Try . . . anything else?"

She shook her head sadly. "People began coming," she said. "Mr. Orlando from the barber shop brought a lantern. All I could see then was Johnny lying there, dead, without his hat. His back . . ."

Crockett cut in, frowning slightly. "Was Johnny wearing his sombrero when you saw him? In the store?"

"Yes," she said. "Yes, he was wearing a hat. I'm sure of that."

For a full minute Crockett stood in silence. He'd hoped for some definite fact that the killer had been one of Gould's own gunmen: Brazos, or possibly Jason. But the missing hat almost completely ruled them out. It meant the killer needed tangible proof he'd done the job. It meant his brother was probably murdered for the reward by a bushwhacker who'd be very careful to claim his money on the sly.

He exhaled deeply, thinking of the hundred desperate men here in Hobart. He turned slowly to leave.

"What are you going to do?" she said, watching him.

"All I can do for now," he said hoarsely. "I'm taking Johnny home to bury him."

When Crockett came out of the store, he saw that Johnny's body had already been moved to Doc Ford's. The yard was quiet now, with only a few people remaining, exchanging their last words on the shooting. They stood out clearly in the bright, almost full moon high above the cottonwoods. Crockett paused by the corner of the building, taking one final glance at the spot where his brother had been killed. The faint prairie night wind coming down the alleyway felt cool to him, chilling after the heat inside the store.

Turning his back to the yard, Crockett walked toward Pioneer. He swung west on the boardwalk for the doctor's house. He'd moved less than twenty feet when he heard the call from behind him.

"Wait, Ruel. Wait a minute!"

Crockett swung around, stepping back into the shadows. In the wide band of lamplight streaming down from the barber shop window, he saw the small coatless, white-shirted figure of Pitkin Allison hurrying towards him. The old storekeeper, panting for breath, came to a wheezing stop.

"Ruel, maybe it'd be better if you kept inside a while," he said. "I've got room in my place if . . ."

"I'm going to see Doc," Crockett told him. "He'll want to see me about the kid."

"That can wait," Allison said. "There are people here who might use the shooting for an excuse to get after you." He gestured behind him at his yard. "There was talk against you, Ruel. They think Johnny'd be alive now if you hadn't tried to hold your land."

Crockett shook his head sadly. "If they think that way, staying inside isn't going to help anything." He started along the walk again.

Allison stood without moving for a few seconds, then followed after the tall cowman. "No, Ruel, wait!" he called.

"Go back to your store, Mr. Allison," said Crockett over his shoulder.

He hadn't expected the people here to let their hate
go this far. Hadn't they learned anything from watching Johnny and himself during all those years before
the war? Hadn't they seen him with his brother these
last couple of days? They'd seen, but they'd missed
everything—the closeness, the feeling of a family building up again. He walked faster, his boot heels thudding
loudly on the plank walk, his face frowning, dejected.

In Gould's dimly lit office Brazos stood tensed at the
window, staring at Crockett's retreating figure.

"Get away from there, Brazos. Don't get any ideas
about Crockett now," Gould growled from the back of
the room.

"I could have finished everything right here and
now. You know damn well I could . . ."

"Yes, I know," Gould cut in furiously. "And everyone in Texas would tie us in with the Crocketts. Your
killing that man out there now could get people thinking."

"Talk about dead men," snorted Brazos, "don't hurt
no one."

"Crockett'll blame me for putting up the reward and
indirectly killing his brother. If I let you go it would
make it just a grudge. The last thing I want is to be
connected with the Crocketts in a feud. No reason for
it, no reason at all."

Brazos laughed and went to the desk and took John-
ny Crockett's sombrero out of the bottom drawer.
"There's a reason for Crockett to have a grudge, amigo.
You keep this. I'm waiting, any time you decide."

Franklin Gould stared down at the hat in silence,
his forehead wrinkled.

Brazos walked around the desk and stopped close to
Gould. "Them posters said two thousand," he said,
holding out his hand. "Two thousand, Mister Gould!"

Pitkin Allison had remained standing in the center
of Pioneer. He'd watched Crockett get himself under
control and then continue on down to Doc Ford's. Allison was one of those frontier men who believed in a man
always doing his duty, and he felt he owed something

to Ruel Crockett. It was something that Pitkin Allison meant to carry to his own grave, something that made him now still try to make things easier for Ruel Crockett.

Allison pushed his way past the Casino's batwings, stopped once inside to look around. The smoke-filled saloon was cool, smelling of stale beer and tobacco. The shaded overhanging lamps threw dark shadows over the men crowding the bar, but even in the dimness he spotted the man he was looking for right away.

Actually, he spotted Jason Dobey first. The huge cowhand, his bandaged nose making him easy to pick out from the other customers, had taken over the far end of the bar, his immense hunched shoulders filling the entire corner. Standing on Jason's right side next to the wall was Fred Hardin.

Allison worked his way along the bar, nodding to men he knew, listening to the talk. The killing seemed to be the only topic of conversation. Everyone was telling his feelings about it with an "I think" or "We should" or a blurting of curses for the bushwhacker. By the time Allison finally reached the rear, Fred Hardin had noticed him coming and slid a bottle along the counter, pointing to a glass.

"Drink, Pit'n," he said drunkenly. "Have one, Pit'n."

"Fred," said Allison, "Johnny Crockett was killed just now."

Jason Dobey grunted, annoyed. "We heard 'bout it, on'y we're drinkin' now."

"Ruel's gone down to Doc's, Fred," said Allison, without so much as a glance at Jason. "He might need some help taking Johnny back home."

Hardin had started to take a drink from his bottle, but he hesitated. The thin red lines of his face seemed to widen as he stared at Allison. "He got shot, huh? John got shot?"

"Yes, Fred. Why don't you go down and help Ruel? Just be there with him?"

For a moment Hardin kept staring. Then his drink-swollen face became truculent. "Ruel don' want me. He don' need me."

"Yes, he does. Your being there will help."

"Shut up, storekeeper," Jason said. He clenched his big fists, glowering. "Leave Fred 'lone."

"What do you say, Fred?" said Allison. He took hold of Hardin's arm, as if to help him walk.

"Let him go!" The voice of Brazos Helm was low, coming from behind Allison.

Allison glanced sideways. Brazos was staring at him, his face strained and intent. He stood beside Jason, his back to the corner so he faced all the doors, just as he always placed himself in any room he entered.

"Go ahead, storekeeper," Brazos said, "get outta here like Jason says."

"Come on, Fred," said Allison. He tugged once at Hardin's sleeve.

"Let go his arm," Brazos warned softly. His fist rose toward Allison's hand.

"I'll get down," Hardin said fast. "You go 'head, Pit'n."

"You sure, Fred?"

"I'll git down. I'll git down."

Brazos spoke, his voice still low pitched, but the hard rasp still there. "You goin', storekeeper?"

Allison looked at Hardin. "You be sure now, Fred," he said. He turned and started walking back along the bar.

"That storekeeper's gonna learn," Brazos said to Jason. "Him an' that cowhand kid of his'll learn damn fast."

Hardin raised the bottle to his lips and drained it. He squared his shoulders. "I'm goin'—" he began.

"Limpy, you're goin' no place," Jason said, straightening his enormous body menacingly.

The small old man wet his lips, began to turn.

"Go 'head," Brazos said. "Try it."

Hardin shot a glance at the gunman. Fright made sweat break out on his flushed forehead. "I wanna help Ruel Crockett," he said.

"You're gonna help him," Brazos said. "You 'n' me are ridin' out to Diamond C. You're gonna do some diggin', amigo."

Fred Hardin backed away from the gunman. "No ...no!"

Brazos looked at Jason. "Gould wants you to find the Allison kid," he said. "Get him over to his office now." Then he took Hardin's arm. "You and me are goin' together, amigo."

"No," Hardin muttered. He swayed as if about to fall, but the strength in Brazos' arm held him up.

Brazos began moving him toward the back door.

Chapter Eleven

CROCKETT spent a long time that evening talking to Doctor Ford, getting all the funeral arrangements straightened out before spending a restless night in the doctor's guest room. Doc would handle everything here in town, while Crockett was to get things ready at Diamond C. Crockett was up before dawn, and he put ten miles of prairie behind him by the time the orange rim of the sun rose above the cloudless line of the eastern horizon.

He saw the smoke first, three uneven thin spirals winding lazily into the blue away off to the southwest.

A frown creased his face as he spurred his mount hard. King answered with a burst of speed, his long legs reaching out, kicking up quick puffs of dust that hung in the air for a while, then settled like flurries of powder on the parched grass.

Forty-five minutes later, his fears were verified. Even at a distance he could see that all the ranch buildings were nothing but smouldering ruins. Soon he could make out figures of people waiting in the yard. Horses were staked out in the oak grove. Crockett slowed his mount, and took the Colt from its holster. He checked the load, then, returning the weapon to his side, pulled the Henry repeater from its boot.

He rode on, keeping the rifle ready across the pommel of his saddle. But he slid the weapon back into place when he saw the people waiting ahead wore the blue uniforms of Federal cavalry. He counted seven soldiers and a civilian he knew was Bol Taylor. Beyond the burned buildings, sitting alone by the corral, was Fred Hardin. He was unmistakable from his slumped, dejected posture.

Unmistakable also was the absence of the longhorns that had been grazing here yesterday. Crockett wasn't surprised at that. Burning and rustling almost naturally went together these days.

He cut through the oak grove. The ring of shod hoofs on rock was loud as he approached the waiting men. He studied the ruins distastefully. One wall of the house remained, but the inside was a mass of charred, smoking timbers. The fire had spread behind the gutted ruins of the barn, leaving only scorched flat for twenty or thirty yards. In the center of the burned-out ground, a pile of fresh-dug earth was brown against the black.

Reining in, Crockett stared at the new grave and the two blackened gravestones to the left of it. He dismounted, weariness stone-heavy on him.

Bol Taylor walked toward him, followed by a lanky red-faced officer wearing the bars of a first lieutenant. The marshal was solemn as he came to a stop.

"Bad thing, Ruel," he said, nodding at the destruction. "Bad about Johnny, too."

"You were hunting him, Bol."

The Federal officer said, "We might've taken him prisoner, though." He frowned, added, "I'm Lieutenant Cahoon. I wish your brother had let us take him."

Crockett nodded but said nothing.

Lieutenant Cahoon glanced back at the ruins. "It was burning when we got here. There wasn't much left to put out. Do you have any idea who could've started it?"

"You want names?" Crockett said curtly.

Cahoon looked Crockett over, ignored the tone of voice. "If you're certain who did it, yes."

Bol Taylor said, "Careful, Ruel. It could've been one of the ranchers who didn't like you coming back. Or maybe they didn't like Gould owning your spread."

Crockett was silent. Cahoon said, "You want to name anyone?"

"No . . . not when I can't be sure," Crockett said.

The officer nodded. Then, still businesslike, "I'm taking my detail up to Austin. If you think there's any threat to you, you can come along.''

''I'll stay here for the funeral,'' Crockett said solemnly.

Again the officer nodded. He started back to his troops, followed by Taylor.

Feeling a deep need to talk to someone who'd understand how he felt, Crockett crossed the yard to where Fred Hardin sat. From behind him he could hear the rattle of equipment and squeak of rigging as the cavalry troops swung aboard. He stopped in front of the old horse wrangler and saw right away he had been drinking heavily, even this morning.

''You dug the grave, Fred?'' he asked.

''Yes. I came out early this mornin'. I figgered I should do it for Johnny. Look, Ruel, I . . .'' His bloodshot eyes flicked toward the sound of footsteps behind Crockett, and he became silent. Looking around, Crockett saw that the Army detail was moving past the live oak grove at a lope. Bol Taylor had remained, and now the marshal stepped in beside him.

''You don't mind if I wait around, Ruel?'' he said. ''I'd like to pay my last respects, too.''

Crockett nodded. He kept looking down at the old man, but Hardin wouldn't meet his eyes. Crockett took out his pipe, began to fill it, still watching Hardin. Shortly, he said, ''You got any idea who fired this place, Fred?''

Hardin wet his lips, glanced at Bol Taylor. Hardin rubbed his hands together nervously, uncomfortably, as though he were waiting for the marshal to speak.

''You didn't see anyone ride off, did you, Fred?'' Crockett said.

''No.'' Hardin's voice was pinched, tense. He would look only at the dusty ground.

The marshal said, ''Fred got here just before we did, Ruel. He had no way of seeing anyone.''

Striking a sulphur match with his thumbnail, Crockett put it to his pipe. He nodded, said to Hardin, ''Thanks for coming out and getting things ready, Fred. I certainly appreciate it.''

Hardin said nothing, just stared down at the ground.

It would be hours before anyone would get out here from Hobart, Crockett knew. Suddenly, he left Hardin and the marshal and walked back to where he'd left his horse.

Mounting, he reined to the left and rode at a jog past the corral. He made a wide circle, east around to west, and then south. All this time he kept leaning over in the saddle, running his eyes across the grass. And, less than a mile south of the gutted ranch buildings, he found what he was looking for.

The thick turf had kept the longhorns' hoofs from cutting into the ground much, but the wide swath of trampled grass told him the gather had been made right here. Some time during the night, he judged, six, maybe seven hours ago.

He moved the gelding along slowly, still leaning down from the saddle, his face grim. The broken, trampled grass made a clear trail a man could follow.

For another half hour he rode that way, going south along the timber-lined flat. He found the signs he wanted, horse signs. After carefully studying the marks of shod hoofs cut plainly in the turf, he knew that there were three horsemen who'd taken his herd.

Back at the corral, he told Bol Taylor. The lawman nodded his head.

"Could be some hands sent out by Gould," he told Crockett. "I can't go after them until I see him about it."

"They're my cattle, Bol. They were branded after Gould stole my mortgage."

"No use getting in a fight over it," Taylor said. "It'll get straightened out in court." He hesitated, his mustached face asking for understanding. Then he added, "I'd only be sticking my neck out if I went after some of Gould's riders. You know that."

Crockett let it go for the present, but impatience prodded him. He'd begin tracking right after the funeral. Three men weren't too many to go after alone.

After the solemn funeral the little group of thirty or so broke up slowly and began to drift away. The majority of the mourners went directly to their horses or wagons and started back just as they'd come, but a few of the people stopped beside Crockett and spoke low words of sympathy. Among them was Pitkin Allison. But Crockett noticed with a feeling of hurt that Janet went directly back to the storekeeper's buggy. The last in line was Marion Howells. He had sensed her eyes watching him as he acknowledged the words of others. When she reached him, her eyes were wet, sincere.

"People spoke so well of your brother," she said, her voice trembling as if she were ashamed of something. "I'm so very sorry, Ruel."

He nodded.

"William never intended for this to happen," she said presently. "You've got to believe that, Ruel."

"It wasn't really your brother's fault," he said. Beyond them, one by one, the wagons and buggies were turning and going from the yard. Only two men remained at the grave: Fred Hardin, who was bent over shoveling the last of the dirt back into place, and Bol Taylor.

Crockett noticed how some of the departing mourners glanced his way, their eyes resting on Marion reprovingly, then on himself. He stiffened and offered his arm to her.

"I'll walk you back to your buggy," he said.

Her dark eyes lifted to his warmly. "I'd like you to, Ruel. Thank you."

They walked to the vehicle without speaking. Her nearness brought a warmth to him, and the feeling was good.

He held her arm while she climbed up onto the seat. She took the reins, but did not shake them. She looked down at him.

"You'll be coming into Hobart," she said. "Come and see us. Please, Ruel?"

"I will," he said.

She smiled, her lovely face relaxing momentarily. Then she gave the reins a slight shake, and the matched bays began to turn.

Marshal Taylor left the grave now and walked to Crockett's side. "You going back to town, Ruel?" His voice was casual, not demanding.

"No. I'm going to see about my cattle."

Taylor's forehead creased. "Don't push any trouble, Ruel," he said. He raised one hand slightly toward the grave. "That's bad enough without making it worse."

When Crockett remained silent, Taylor added, "I'll take Fred back with me. If it's all right with you."

Crockett nodded, then walked to where he'd staked out his horse in the oak grove. By the time he'd finished saddling the animal, Taylor and Fred Hardin were already out on the flat heading east. Crockett mounted and sat quietly, watching them go for several minutes.

Then he kneed King easily and turned him south.

Crockett traveled steadily, finding the trail easy to follow. He kept his horse moving at a lope, sometimes in a long-reaching trot, his hard eyes always on the trampled broken grass.

The horsemen ahead had taken absolutely no action to hide their trail. Here in the low hills they probably had no fear of anyone coming on them undetected.

Even in the thickening dusk the trail soon seemed to become plainer. Crockett slowed down, his eyes squinting against the darker shadows, nervously searching the skyline and every piece of timber, every patch of brush as he rode along.

The sound of bawling cattle floated back to him through the half-darkness before he actually saw the cows. Instantly he pulled up, his hand tight and sweaty on the reins, his knee pressed hard to the good feel of the sheathed Henry under his leg.

Only a few seconds passed before the bawling reached him again, a bawling with the particular sound that told him the cattle weren't being driven. Quickly, he dismounted. He led King back the way he'd come, ready to cover the horse's nostrils at any sign that he might whinny or nicker. Five hundred yards back he tied the animal to a pin oak tree. Then, Henry in hand, he went ahead again, angling to the left so he'd come up in the thick underbrush there.

Keeping to the brush this way he got close enough to see the cattle clearly in the shadowed moonlight, bedded down for the night in a meadow-like stretch running down to a small creek. A campfire flickered close to the creek bank, beyond three bunched-together animals.

Impatience prickled Crockett, but judgment held him back. He moved through the brush slowly and bellied down under a thick, low-growing mesquite. But he was still too far away to see any movement at the fire.

He crouched again and started ahead. He had gone only five feet when something alerted him, some indefinite flutter of movement between himself and the campfire. He threw his body forward, slamming to the ground.

The blast of the shot racketed across the clearing. The bullet ripped the air inches above his head, whacking solidly into a tree behind him. Then, silence followed.

Crockett lay there flat on his belly, tensely holding the Henry ready, sweating as he listened for any sound of movement from the men he was hunting.

Chapter Twelve

CATTLE PLODDED about the meadow, terrified, stampeding by instinct away from the shooting. Crockett's hesitation lasted only the length of time it took to breathe. Before the rifle pounded again from ahead, he was moving, crawling deeper into the cover of the brush.

The second bullet whined, whacked into one of the running cows with the noise of a loud handslap. The animal screamed and went down kicking.

Again the rifle roared, the bullet zinging past the spot Crockett had just left. He had this one gunman spotted from the flash of the barrel, but he didn't dare shoot. One blast from the Henry and they'd all know where he was.

Maybe that was their plan: to have one of them draw his fire, allowing the others to open up.

In bitter despair Crockett, still crouching low, moved to the cover of a giant oak. He'd had the opportunity for a surprise attack, but he'd let it slide through his hands like water. They would be spreading out, hemming him in. If he ran maybe he could get away, maybe not. But if he ran, he'd not get another chance at them.

Out in the clearing the cow was still screaming. To Crockett it was a thick, piercing bellow. There was no other sound but the night wind rustling the leaves above.

A shadow moved fifty yards away, between him and the campfire. He watched the deep darkness. Knowing the time for taking a chance had come, he raised the rifle, balancing it on his palm. He separated the target from the trunks of trees, judged the distance and shot high.

The gunman's rifle blasted into the air, almost drowning out the shocked, shrill scream the man emitted. Crockett made his dash, keeping low, throwing his body down to escape the expected hail of bullets.

None came.

The echo of the shot died to almost complete quiet, the silence broken by two sounds now, the dying grunts of the cow in the meadow, the groaning and gasping of a man.

Crockett's hands were icy. He waited for someone to go to the wounded man, for someone to call out. But nothing happened.

After two minutes Crockett held the Henry out at arm's length and shot into the air, dropping back fast so the drawn fire wouldn't hit him.

When no gunfire came, he waited another minute, then inched his way toward the sound of the wounded man's groaning.

The man lay near the fire, his rifle beyond his grasp. He was still gasping and mumbling incoherently, one hand pressed tightly to his chest.

Crockett held the Henry ready in case the wounded man tried to use a hand gun. He remained in a half-crouch as he walked closer. The man rolled onto his left side and in the flickering firelight Crockett could see the dark stain of blood on his chest and side. Then, he glimpsed the pain-twisted face. It was Ben Allison.

Ben had heard him approach. He stared up, hate mixed with pain in his eyes. His gaze stopped on Crockett's rifle.

"Go 'head . . . shoot." He cursed, straining to get the words out.

"Where are the others?" Crockett said.

Suddenly Ben rolled to the left and grabbed for his rifle. Crockett's foot shot out, kicked the weapon clear of the reaching fingers. Ben swore violently, then, moaning, bent double from pain. Crockett leaned over him and slid his six-gun from its holster.

"Who were the others?" Crockett asked coldly. "Brazos? Jason?"

Ben mumbled an obscene Spanish curse. "I hope they kill you," he said, spitting the words through clenched teeth. "I hope they kill you hard." He shuddered and pressed both hands to his chest.

Dropping to his knees, Crockett reached for Ben's hands. Ben swung out with his fist, just missing Crockett's chin. Crockett slapped the beardless face hard with his open palm. Ben fell back and cursed again.

"You young fool," Crockett snapped. "If I don't stop that bleeding, you'll die."

"You'll let me die anyway," Ben sneered.

"Maybe I should," Crockett said without emotion. "But your father has lost too much already."

Ben lay still, breathing deeply, his glare changing a little, but the hate was still there. Crockett parted Ben's clenched hands, then opened the shirt. A lot of blood had been spilled already; even the jeans were soaked.

Ben's pressing hands had almost stopped the bleeding, and now only a thin trickle came from the wound.

The bullet had gone in high, into the flesh below the shoulder, and had ripped out at the back. Crockett pressed along the side to see if a rib had been nicked. Ben whimpered, stiffening his body. He stared up at Crockett, his eyes clouded, brimming with tears of pain and frustration.

"I'll have to fire that to stop infection," Crockett said. "Cigarette?"

Ben's face grimaced as he understood. He shook his head. "Get it over with. Quick."

With care, Crockett dragged him closer to the fire and put more kindling on so he could see better. He found the pan Ben had used as a coffee pot. After emptying the grounds, he got water from the creek and heated it. He found a flour sack in Ben's saddlebags, washed it and hung it close to the fire to dry. Then he went to work picking the threads of shirt out of the wound.

Half-conscious with pain and exhaustion, Ben lay back, clenching his teeth so he wouldn't cry out. Crockett stepped back to the fire after he was through cleaning the wound. He kept his side between the boy and the six-gun barrel he was heating red-hot over the flames. He realized in the complete silence that the cow in the meadow was dead.

Ben's lips began shaking when Crockett returned with the pistol.

"Sorry I haven't any whisky," Crockett said.

Nodding slowly, Ben clenched his teeth. He breathed hard, sweated, groaned as the barrel hit the wound. Then, mercifully, he fainted. Crockett worked fast, sickened by the smell of burned flesh. He finished cauterizing and had the sack bandage on long before Ben came around.

Mumbling incoherently, Ben opened his eyes. His gaze rested on Crockett and he remembered. He saw too that Crockett had brought his own gelding up from where he'd left it along the trail.

"Smoke?" said Crockett. When the boy nodded, he slid one of the cigarettes he'd made up into Ben's mouth and lit it.

Ben inhaled deeply and let the smoke drift out. "You could've left me here," he said presently.

Crockett nodded to the steaming can over the fire. "Coffee?" he said.

"Yes." Ben tried to push himself up onto his good elbow, but he fell back and lay there shakily.

The boy was watching Crockett, considering him, his beardless face softer now.

"Brazos and Jason drove these cattle with me," he volunteered.

"And they left you here alone?"

Ben nodded. "We figured you'd pick up the trail. I

was waitin' for you to show up since this afternoon. I was supposed to kill you when you came up. I'd only be protectin' Mr. Gould's cattle when I done it.''

''You think they planned it that way, Ben?''

''That was it. But . . .''

Crockett's hard words cut in. ''They staked you out, Ben. Everyone knows there's a grudge between us. If I killed you, then Gould could get the army after me.''

Ben stared at him, his wide eyes filled with understanding now.

''They figured it would end that way,'' Crockett added. ''That's why they made you stay here alone.''

Quickly Ben shook his head. ''They didn't make me stay,'' he said bitterly. ''I wanted to stay.'' His voice softened. ''You can see why I . . .''

''Yes. I see,'' Crockett said. ''You get rested now, so we can get back. Go ahead, kid. You rest now.''

It was after nine the next morning when Crockett walked the horses slowly into the yard behind Allison's store. Ben was half-conscious, bent over in the saddle, gripping the horn to keep erect. Down through the alleyway, Crockett noticed the usual morning activity of buggies, wagons and riders along Pioneer with bonneted women moving along the walks.

It was when he was untying Ben from the saddle of the roan and helping him to the ground that he became aware of the two men who had stopped at the far end of the alley, watching him.

Ben stumbled, barely able to keep his legs under him.

''Easy . . . easy,'' Crockett told him. Ben held on tightly, and before they'd reached the store's back entrance, Pitkin Allison had thrown the door open.

''Good Lord! What happened?'' the storekeeper cried hoarsely.

''I got shot,'' Ben said, swallowing against the pain in his body.

''Shot?'' the gray-haired old man said in a soft horrified voice. He came close, supported his son's other side. ''How did you find him, Ruel?''

''I shot him, Mr. Allison,'' Crockett said.

The old man halted, quickly and involuntarily, as if

the shock of the words had floored him. "No . . . no," he said, breathing the words softly. "You wouldn't—"

"Wasn't Ruel's fault," Ben mumbled. "I'll tell you, Pa."

Allison grew silent, his face pale. As they moved Ben into the building, the boy blurted out most of what had happened.

They sat Ben in a chair inside the store's back room. Crockett checked for bleeding. Only a little blood had escaped during the long ride. Allison stood motionless, holding his son upright, watching with a white, quiet face. Crockett looked up when the door behind him opened and Janet Bankhead started through the doorway.

She stopped short. "No . . . ," she said. "Not Ben too?"

"Get the doctor," Crockett told her. "He needs Doc."

She stood there in silence, staring at him. Then, she said, "You shot him?"

"Get the doctor," Crockett repeated coldly.

Suddenly she started forward, raising one arm to strike him. "Hateful . . . hateful," she cried, beginning to weep now. "You kill everything you touch. You—"

He stood, pulling back an inch to dodge her slap, then, grabbing her frail shoulders in his big hands, shook her.

"Ben needs the doctor," he snapped. "Can't you see that?"

She came out of her hysteria instantly, stared at his face.

"Get over to Doc's," he ordered. "Tell him Ben can't be moved."

"Yes," she whispered, "I'll go."

He released his grip, turning her as he did so. She went out through the doorway.

Crockett faced Pitkin Allison. "Where would Jason and Brazos be now?" His voice had suddenly turned stone-hard.

Allison scarcely heard the question. "Ben's bad hurt," he muttered. "Stay here until Doc—"

"You can handle him 'til he comes. Where do they live?"

The old man, looking into Crockett's savage face, recoiled. "Don't go after them," he cried. "They'll kill you!"

"This kid's dying because of them. You see what they made me do?"

"But—"

"Where are they?"

"I—" Allison exhaled wearily, stared down at his son. "Brazos would be with Gould in his office. Jason ... maybe in the Casino."

Crockett turned on his heel and started out.

Standing there, Allison was silent, watching. He looked at his son again, tightened his wrinkled hands on the boy's shoulders. As he glanced toward the sound of the back door closing behind Crockett, a slow chill seeped through his body, and he shuddered.

Chapter Thirteen

OUTSIDE, Crockett saw that men had begun to congregate in the small yard. The crowd backed up, making a path for him along the alleyway. More people, some of them women and children, were coming toward the general store. Word had spread like fire through cured grass about his bringing Ben Allison in half dead.

Pioneer Street was darkly shadowed under the clouding sky. Crockett felt the coolness of the wind on his cheek, recognized the advancing damp and sweet smell of approaching rain.

He knocked loudly on the door of Gould's office and, after that, walked around the building peering into the windows. He made certain that no one was inside. Then he crossed quickly to the Casino.

Gil Caldwell's practiced bartender's eye spotted Crockett the second he pushed through the batwings. Crockett halted directly opposite him. Seeing the hard expression on Crockett's face, the skinny bartender momentarily stopped wiping the counter.

"Brazos Helm or Jason in here?" Crockett asked loudly.

One blue-veined hand went to the bartender's chin. "Ain't seen neither of 'em."

But Crockett had noticed how the three men standing at the bar had stiffened. "Where are they?" he asked.

Caldwell stared back at him, his face showing nothing. One of the drinkers flicked a glance at the door to the back room. Crockett caught that and began heading for the door. Caldwell leaned across the counter, reached out with one hand and caught Crockett's shirt sleeve. A slight jerk of Crockett's arm broke the bartender's grip.

"I don't want no trouble," whined Caldwell. "I don't like Jason no better'n you, but he's Gould's . . ."

"It's Jason who's in there?" said Crockett, aware of the tight stillness in the long room.

"Yuh. Look, Ruel. I can't stand havin' trouble with Gould's men."

"This isn't your trouble," Crockett said flatly and continued on past the tables to the door.

Jason Dobey, sitting at a table eating alone, lifted his big head as Crockett shoved the door open. Only one hanging lamp lighted the room, and the shadows were thick at the doorway. For a moment Jason sat there, the knife he used as others would use a fork poised in the air, his initial irritated stare gradually changing to a wide frown. Unconsciously, he fingered the bandage crowning his nose.

"What you want?" he asked sullenly.

"I found my herd last night, Jason."

The immense cowhand jabbed the knife impatiently into the thick steak that entirely filled his plate. "Don't bother me with your troubles," he said, biting at the meat.

"The Allison kid was waiting for me." Slowly Crockett walked closer to the table. "We're going to talk about how he got there."

"You go 'head and talk. I'm eatin'." He waved at a chair with a bear-sized hand. When the hand dropped, it went beneath the table, out of sight.

"Go ahead," Crockett said softly. "Give me a reason."

Jason stopped his vigorous chewing. His black eyes

held something close to fear as he laid the knife down and leaned his powerful shoulders back as though he intended to stand.

"Go ahead," Crockett snapped, his tone hopeful. "Give me a chance. One chance, Jason."

The giant paused as fear completely claimed him. Watching Crockett, he knew he was a dead man if he made another move.

Neither man spoke for a moment, both motionless in the deep-shadowed room. Then Crockett said, "You were out there with Ben?"

"Brazos asked me to help drive the cows," Jason blurted. He brought both hands up, laid them flat on the table. He watched Crockett carefully. "They were Mr. Gould's cows."

"You left the kid out there all alone?"

"Sure. All we did was drive 'em where they could have good grazin'." He spoke slowly, never taking his eyes from Crockett's face. "We was goin' t' pick 'em up in the rodeo later on."

"Don't give me that," Crockett said, controlling his words with difficulty. "You left the kid out there to bushwhack me."

"No . . . no, we didn't. We just drove 'em to a good meadow. If Ben says any different he's lyin'. It's my word 'gainst his. Me an' Brazos—"

"Where's Brazos?"

Jason smiled cautiously. "He dropped off at the Peterson's. They got a little Mex cook he's been—"

"He coming in today?"

"I don't know. Sometimes he stops two, three days." The smile was gone.

Crockett leaned forward, resting the palms of his hands inches from Jason's. His voice was soft, a strange, tense smile playing on his lips.

"Get out of Hobart," he said. "You're through here. Get out. You hear me?"

Jason hesitated.

Crockett hit him immediately, his doubled fist smashing low on the wide cheek. The impact of the blow straightened Jason and knocked him sprawling over the back of the chair.

"You hear me?" Crockett repeated.

"Yuh . . . yuh! I'll get out! I'll get out!"

Crockett began backing towards the door slowly. Jason got to his feet, holding one huge hand against the ugly red mark on his face.

Closing the door behind him, Crockett walked past the tables. Gil Caldwell and the drinkers at the bar had been staring at the door when he came out. He was almost opposite the near end of the bar when the expressions on the watchers' faces changed abruptly. Crockett heard the low snap of a latch clicking behind him. As he turned, he threw himself to the left, crashing into a table and taking it down with him.

Jason's immense frame was silhouetted blackly in the doorway, the lamplight behind him glaring out into the bar as he fired desperately, once, twice.

The round top of the table took the bullets meant for Crockett. Still rolling, Crockett brought up the .44, steadied it and thumbed the hammer. Roaring concussion knocked Crockett still more off balance.

Crockett's bullet struck Jason's right cheek, ripping a deep bloody gash, but the giant kept coming. Swaying, he slowed scant feet away, dropping his six-gun low.

Crockett squeezed the trigger again and again, methodically. Then, in a whipping motion, he rolled to the right.

He heard the blast of Jason's Colt, felt the shock as the whirring bullet split the pine floor where he'd been lying. Crockett lay on his stomach and aimed his revolver.

Jason's bulky shape shook behind the wreath of gunsmoke. The giant tottered and plunged forward, hitting the overturned table with a bone-crunching thud.

Crockett sprang to his feet and advanced toward the prostrate form. Jason didn't move. Cautiously, Crockett turned the huge man over with the toe of his boot, and he saw that Jason Dobey was dead.

The sound of running boots and excited talk bounced in from the porch. Crockett peered over the batwings. It seemed to have become very dark outside, and he knew the cloudiness wouldn't help his vision if Brazos was among those attracted by the shooting.

He knew there'd be no time to reload the cap-and-ball revolver. He kept his back to the wall as he checked the cylinder of the Colt to see that the three remaining caps in the tubes hadn't become disengaged during the scuffle with Jason.

Men's watching faces were lined over the tops of the swinging doors. A few had crouched down so they could see from underneath. Men stood beyond the porch, and some were crossing the street towards the saloon. Bol Taylor, with his forearms folded into a wedge, battered his way through the crowd, shoving men aside in brutal haste. He pushed through the batwings and came straight toward Crockett.

Al Cox followed only a step behind the marshal. Immediately, the young deputy spread his long arms across the doorway. "Back up! Back outside!" he shouted at the surging crowd.

Marshal Taylor's eyes moved from the ready Colt in Crockett's hand to Jason Dobey's body. His mustached mouth tightened.

"Well, Ruel," he said tensely, "what happened?" He kept his hand ready above his own gun, as though he expected trouble.

"Jason jumped him," one of the cowhands at the bar said. He spoke fast, blurted out what had happened.

Taylor listened, waiting with his stiff-legged stance, his eyes not leaving Crockett. While the cowhand talked, Crockett watched the faces of the other witnesses. There was no hostility toward him, but neither was there friendliness.

"That all?" Taylor asked when the cowhand finished.

"No more," the man answered emphatically. "Jason damn well won't bully anyone else in this town."

The lawman nodded. "Self-defense," he said soberly. "But there'll be an inquest. You stay around, Ruel."

"I'll be here for any inquest," Crockett said.

Crockett headed toward Allison's back yard, where he'd left his horse. Men stood in groups along the walks, some of them angry-looking, reluctant to give way to him. He knew they weren't all here just because of the shooting. The cowhands inside the Casino hadn't shown any of the hatred he saw here. Crockett slowed his step.

The sky had completely clouded over, and by the time

Crockett reached the alleyway between the general store and the barber shop, he felt the first drop of rain. He was thinking of the long ride to the Peterson ranch, but the promise of rain didn't bring any change in his decision to go after Brazos.

He was close to the end of the alley when three men moved out from behind Allison's store. One of them covered him with an old Harper's Ferry musket.

A voice behind him snarled, "Right there . . . stop right there, Crockett!"

He whirled on his heel, pressing the flat of his back against the rough clapboards of the building. Bob De-Witt came toward him, his short bantam-legged body crouched, the bandage circling his head gray in the clouded daylight.

"You shot young Ben, huh?" DeWitt sneered.

Men crowding in behind the stubby cowhand blocked any hope of escape. Shock froze Crockett, recollection of the beating a mob like this had given him rushing to his brain. His hand dropped to his Colt, every muscle of his body rigid.

"Don't . . ." the man with the Harper's Ferry warned.

Crockett saw hand guns appear in the fists of the converging men. They came closer, their faces terribly grim in the silence.

DeWitt waved a thick arm at a nearby cowhand. "Get his gun," he ordered.

Chapter Fourteen

SLOWLY the cowhand stepped forward and edged around to Crockett's right. An uneasy snicker ran through the crowd as Crockett shoved the man's reaching hand away. The momentary attention Crockett gave to the cowhand had been enough for DeWitt to spring ahead and throw the first punch.

The stinging blow landed on the side of Crockett's head, knocking off his sombrero, driving him flush against the building. He brought both hands up to defend himself as another man's fist struck. He tried to duck away, to keep his balance, but couldn't. A hand tugged at his holster, and the Colt was jerked clear. The throng pressed in on him, smashing, pushing, shoving at each other to get at him, all worked up to lynch-mob fury now.

A chopping fist pounded all feeling from Crockett's neck, another scraped skin from his cheek. Crockett lunged forward, trying to break through those swarming in from the right, but a vicious smash to his stomach blasted the air from his lungs.

He reached out, tried to catch hold of something for support. His outstretched fingers were flayed aside, and more fists joined in the pummeling. Falling, he felt himself jerked back to a standing position, heard a shrill rebel yell, the rumbling of excited, hate-filled laughter.

He was pounded to the ground, pulled up again, smashed back to all fours, then thrown to his knees. A wetness ran across his face, warm and sticky, and he gulped in the salty taste of his own blood. Then he was on the ground, and the yelling seemed a long way off. A blurry figure bent over him, shouting into his face.

"Crockett." The words came to him from a far distance. "Crockett, can you hear me?"

"He c'n hear yuh. . . . He c'n hear yuh," someone yelled.

A hand slapped his face. "Can you hear me?" the question came again.

Crockett wasn't capable of answering. He lay there fighting for air, feeling the knifing pain that came at each breath he drew.

"You get outta Texas, Crockett, y' hear?" the voice said.

Then a loud, shrill, somehow familiar voice sounded through the yelling. "What are you men doing? What are you doing there, DeWitt?"

The shouting began to break off a little at the rear of the mob. Crockett lay sprawled out, but he could see that the feet of those over him were moving back.

"Good Lord," the familiar voice said. "Good Lord, what have you men done?" A thin rumble of protest broke from the speaker's throat followed by a loud shuffling of feet.

"Hey . . . hey, watch him!" a voice called. "Watch him!"

Then, "Get back . . . all of you, get back!"

Crockett pushed himself up onto one elbow. Through the tears that stung his eyes, he saw Pitkin Allison standing above him, holding an Enfield rifle waist high, aimed and ready.

"Get back," Allison was repeating. "I'll shoot the first one to touch him again."

Bob DeWitt yelled, "He killed Tom! And Ben's dyin' in there! Allison, how can you . . ."

"Ben bushwhacked Crockett," the old man answered. "Brazos and Jason made Ben do it. Crockett saved my boy's life by bringing him back here."

"What 'bout Tom?" someone shouted. Another picked that up, added, "That turncoat shot Tom 'fore he had a chance to draw. You forgettin' that, Pit?"

A roar of agreement went up then, and men pressed closer together, as though they intended to start on Crockett again. All Crockett could do was stay there, slumped on the ground, spitting the blood that flowed from his torn lips. Allison motioned the mob back with a threatening upward jerk of the rifle's muzzle.

"That isn't how it happened." Allison spoke slowly, his voice level. "Tom went after Ruel with his gun drawn. Creed was there. He saw it. He told me that before he died at Palmito Hill. Ruel told the truth at the inquest." He breathed deeply, then added, "Now you know. Now, you know my shame."

Silence fell, dead silence. The sound of feet shuffling in the sand seemed loud. In the quiet Crockett felt a cold wet drop touch his face, then another and another. Even the intermittent patter of the falling rain seemed unusually loud.

Allison bent over Crockett, grasped him by the armpits to help him stand. "Easy . . . easy, Ruel," he said. He straightened again and glanced along the alley. "You stay there, and I'll get somebody to help."

The shouting in the Casino had wakened Fred Hardin from a drunken stupor. He had pushed open the door to the loft of Sutton's blacksmith's shop and looked out. Watching the street, he had followed the movements of everyone in sight these last five minutes. He knew right away when Ruel Crockett came out of the saloon that he'd been in on the gunfight. He knew from the way the town men stood around watching Ruel, then began following him up the alley, that they were after him. His whisky throat burned from not giving the warning he'd wanted to shout.

Hardin had climbed down from the loft and mixed in with the watching men grouped just inside John Sutton's shop, had heard the talk about Ben Allison. Now, as he stared at the throng of men retreating in silence from the alleyway, Hardin felt the burning in his throat gag him. They'd done what they'd meant to do, what they'd been waiting for since Ruel came back. But somehow there wasn't much satisfaction there now, which showed in the low and guarded way they talked, and the way they split up and left each other like all pride in their act was gone.

A man close to Hardin chuckled. "Well now," he said to Sutton and the others, "I reckon we'll see another turncoat Texan ridin' back north where he belongs."

The other men laughed.

Tears, sudden and uncontrollable, came to Hardin's eyes. It would be worse than the last time, he thought, picturing what Ruel had looked like when he'd brought him back to Diamond C. He had to look, had to see what had happened over there. He braced himself, then started with his limping gait from the barn.

Rain hit him, clung to his dirt-streaked rumpled clothing. Wisps of steam rose from each drop that struck the parched dust of the street. Bol Taylor and Gil Caldwell came out of the Casino, followed closely by four men carrying a spread-eagled body. Hardin's pulse slowed when he saw their burden was Jason Dobey. Exhilaration exploded through Hardin, but it started to fade when the marshal waved to him.

"Wait up, Fred," Taylor called, stepping from the porch and heading toward him.

"I'm not doin' anythin', Bol." Hardin caught the lawman's glance at the alleyway, but his face didn't betray what he'd seen. "I'm jest walkin'."

"Then you can come over to Mr. Gould's with me," Taylor said, looking directly into Hardin's eyes. "Gil here was a witness to the shooting. You'll want to hear."

Hardin offered evasively, "You don't need me, Bol."

"I want a third person there when he tells it, Fred. You come along."

Dejection had replaced all exhilaration now. Hardin nodded, following along behind Taylor and the bartender to the steps of Gould's building. Staring down the street, he didn't notice Pitkin Allison as he came running from the alleyway, but his ears caught the storekeeper's yell.

"Fred! Hey, Fred!" Allison's plodding footsteps sounded wetly on the walk as he approached. "Fred, give me a hand with Ruel!"

Halting, Fred Hardin began to turn, but it was Bol Taylor who gave Allison an answer.

"Fred's coming with me," he said. "I need him for something."

Allison came to a wheezing stop, inclined his gray-haired head toward the lawman. "I just want him to help me get Ruel up to Doc's."

"You can get someone else, Pit."

"Who else? They all hate Ruel. And Doc can't leave Ben."

Taylor ignored the reasoning. "No . . ." he began, then hesitated as footsteps sounded and the door behind him opened. Gould stepped outside. The stockman held a pile of papers in one hand.

"What's the matter, Marshal?" he said.

"Jason Dobey was killed in a gunfight just now," Taylor said. "Seeing as he was your hand, I thought you'd like to talk to a witness. I brought Hardin along to see there was no intimidation or anythin'."

Gould nodded. "That seems in order," he said. He glanced from the marshal to Allison and back. "Why all this talk?"

"Some cowhands beat up Ruel Crockett," Allison told him. "Fred's the only one in town who'd be willin' to help me get him to Doc's."

"Hardin works for me now, not for Crockett."

"This has nothing to do with who Fred works for. Ruel needs help. Now."

With a faint smile Gould said, "Well, I need Hardin, too. But if it's worth losing his job for, he can go along with you." He looked at Hardin, waited.

Allison said to Hardin, "Well, Fred?"

They all watched Fred Hardin as he stared down at the ground. His dust-stained clothing was drenched. He looked pathetic standing there, drops of rain glistening in his white hair and running down his wrinkled forehead in little rivulets to hang quivering from nose and chin.

"Well, Fred?" Allison said again. "At least help me get him into my back room?"

Bol Taylor moved close to the old cowhand. "I didn't mean to put you on the spot, Fred. But think now."

Allison said, "I don't see why it's so important that Fred doesn't . . ."

"It's important," Gould said. "If he works for me, it's very important."

Hardin stared up into the stockman's face, then slid his eyes to Taylor. He swayed, as if suddenly chilled by the rain and wind. "I'll go inside," he mumbled. He seemed to shrink inside his sodden clothes while he stared glassily at the mud between his boots.

Allison watched him with a rigid, hopeless expression. Gould said, "We'll talk inside, Marshal." He swung around and led the way into his office.

Inside, Gould sat at the big mahogany desk while Gil Caldwell told about the shooting. Hardin walked to a corner of the room and stood with his back to the bookcase. He looked down at the floor, but his ears were cocked toward the talk like a frightened rabbit.

Gould was thoughtfully silent while the bartender gave his story, not asking any questions until Caldwell had finished. Finally, he said, "And you think Crockett was looking for Brazos, to gun him too?"

"He wanted them both, Mr. Gould. He was hunting for Jason and Brazos."

The stockman answered Caldwell calmly. "Can you keep the talk down? Brazos works for me, and I don't want my hired hands having shootouts over a foolish grudge. You can understand that.''

''Sure . . . sure, Mr. Gould.'' Caldwell's skinny blue-veined hand rubbed at the corner of his mouth. ''I'll tell them cowhands who were inside to keep shut.''

Nodding, Gould said, ''You just tell what happened when they hold the inquest. I agree with the marshal. It looks to me like a case of self-defense.''

''I'm sorry 'bout it happenin' in my place,'' the bartender offered. ''I didn't want . . .''

''That's all right,'' Gould said emphatically. ''I don't hold you responsible.''

He rose and stretched, signifying the talk was over. Then he looked at Hardin. ''You look as though you can use a drink, Fred.'' His hand went into his coat pocket and came out with some silver coins. ''Here, have a couple on me. Go ahead.''

''But you said . . .''

''It's all right. You go along with Caldwell.''

''Yuh. Thanks, Mr. Gould.'' Hardin didn't know what was behind the stockman's blank stare. He felt a surge of fear.

Slithering sideways, he almost bumped into Bol Taylor, who was hurrying from the room.

''Hold it,'' Gould said, and Hardin froze. ''Where will you be if I want you, Fred? The Casino?''

Hardin's head wagged. ''Uh . . . yes. I'm gonna get me a drink.''

Bol Taylor waited until the door was closed behind Hardin before he spoke. ''I don't know about Fred, Mr. Gould. He . . .''

''Don't worry about Limpy,'' said Gould. ''He'll end up so drunk he won't even know when Brazos gets back. He'll be too drunk to realize what happens to Crockett —or himself.''

The final nod from Gould was enough for Hardin to start moving once he was out the door. He half-ran into the drenching rain, and his bobbing gait became more pronounced with his increased speed. Though his throat ached from needing a drink, he drove off the craving for liquor. He gave no thought to Crockett, had no thought but to get out of town.

"They're comin' . . . comin'," he whispered to himself. "They'll come after me now."

He was alone. Alone for the first time in six months. That and the thought of how Gould had looked at him back in the office sobered Hardin completely. He wasn't sure what had caused the change. He wasn't sure that he hadn't known all along that it would come to this. The mud was sticky beneath his boots. It seemed to clutch at him, to hold him back as he crossed toward the blacksmith's.

John Sutton was not inside. He'd probably gone over to the Casino to get in on the excited talk about the gunfight and beating. Hardin dragged his saddle down from where it lay over the top beam of a stall. He saddled his sorrel mare and left by the back door.

Hardin had no idea where he was going. He only knew he had to run, and from habit he headed south. The driving rain was cold against his drenched body. He rode on, feeling the chill penetrating through him, and passed the empty glade that until yesterday had held the Army encampment. As he rode by the half-finished mansion Gould was building, he noticed that no one was working there in the storm, but he gave no further thought to that until he reached the creek.

He was crossing the bridge when the idea of hiding in Gould's house came to him. He pulled in his mount, got some control of himself. They'd never think of looking for him there. He would be out of the storm, would get a chance to dry himself and the horse, and to think.

Once there, Hardin began to calm down. He tied the sorrel in a back stall where the barn roof was already half-finished and where even a sudden whinny could not be heard from the road. Then he went to the large opening that was to be the front door and looked out.

Immediately he spotted the horse and rider coming from Hobart, moving along the road toward the bridge at Hackberry Creek. Even through the falling rain he could tell it was Bol Taylor.

Hardin's wet shirt, plastered against his back, had turned icy, and a shiver ran down his spine. He could not run, could not hope to escape. Panicky, he fell flat, lay there.

In that prone position he watched the marshal ride

past without even a glance toward the buildings. Hardin began to shake from reaction, feeling giddily elated in the knowledge he hadn't been followed. All he had to do was wait until dark, and he could get away.

He watched Taylor until the rider crossed the bridge and swung due north on the flat beyond. Only one ranch lay in that direction—Rube Peterson's spread. He knew too that Gould was sending for Brazos Helm.

For the first time since he'd started to run, Fred Hardin had a thought for someone other than himself. He thought of Ruel Crockett lying beaten and bruised in Allison's back room.

Inside the back room of the general store, Pitkin Allison had been working over Ruel Crockett for the last fifteen minutes. Now, the elderly storekeeper's fingers pressed at the purplish bruise that ran the length of Crockett's left side.

"Nothing broken," he said. He dropped the soggy, bloody towel he'd used to clean the dirt and grime from Crockett's face into a water bucket. "But you've got to get rest ... plenty of rest."

Crockett nodded slightly. Saying nothing, he leaned back in the chair, trying to offset the pain by listening to the steady drumming of rain on the roof. He wasn't a pretty sight, with one eye swollen almost shut and a purplish-black bruise discoloring the right side of his face. His lower lip was so cut and puffed that it lifted his chin and jaw way out of proportion. He drew a long slow breath as Allison dabbed at the blood still trickling from the split lip.

Allison said slowly, "You can use the spare room in my house."

"The hell I will," said Crockett roughly. "You stopped them out there, but they'll want another try. Well, I'll damn well give them their chance."

"No, Ruel, those men won't be after you again. They did wrong out there. Most of them . . ." He stopped talking as quick footsteps approached from inside the store.

The door swung open and Janet Bankhead came hurrying into the room. Her small face was pale and strained, and she was out of breath from running. Crockett glanced at her, then lifted his shirt and took out his sack of tobacco to fashion a cigarette.

"Doctor Ford'll be down as soon as he can," she said. "He still had Ben in his office." She drew a long breath, and as her eyes ran over Crockett's face a little tremor went through her thin body. "Anything I can do to help?"

"No," Crockett said with a tinge of bitterness. "When I need your help I'll ask for it." He gave up the effort to make a smoke and slid the tobacco into his pocket.

"But I . . ." Janet began.

"Get him a shirt from inside," Allison said. When the girl left he added firmly, "There was no reason for that, Ruel. She was only trying to help."

Crockett leaned forward and exhaled wearily, looking down at his bloodied shirt on the floor. The pain that lay in his chest and face made his head throb heavily. His mouth was dry. He remained motionless, hoping that quiet would ease the dull throbbing ache. When Janet returned he tried to stand.

"Sit there, Ruel," said Allison. "The main thing you need now is plenty of rest."

"I'll get rest later," Crockett said testily. Before he got to his feet he felt the dizziness return, and with a grimace of pain he sat again.

He stayed that way for another minute. Janet unfolded the shirt, unbuttoned it and hung it on a chair close to him. Allison busied himself folding muslin into something resembling a bandage. Then the quiet of the room was broken when a loud knocking sounded on the back door.

Crockett straightened, pain slashing through him as he dropped his hand for his Colt. He heard the voice of Fred Hardin calling low but clear. "Ruel . . . you in there, Ruel?"

Allison opened the door, and the old horse wrangler limped in quickly. Water dripped onto the floor from his drenched clothing, making small puddles around his boots.

"You've got to git outta town, Ruel," Hardin said. "You've gotta . . ."

"No. I'll be damned if I run."

"But Gould's sent for Brazos. Brazos'll come after you soon's he hits town." Hardin turned to Allison, pleading for help. "He's in no shape to face anyone, leastwise a gunhand like Brazos. You can see that."

"Brazos comes, I'll face him," Crockett said quietly.

"You wouldn't stand a chance," Allison said. "Fred's right. You can hide in my . . ."

"I've got a place," Hardin said, then went on to tell about where he'd been hiding. "I took a chance leavin' there, but I hadda warn you, Ruel. I hadda warn you."

"Yes," Allison said. "It's the best thing. You'll have the whole night to rest." He looked at Janet. "Get some blankets, and food. . . . They'll need slickers, too. And a lantern."

Hardin said, "Hurry up, Ruel. We wait 'til this rain stops, they'll see us."

Crockett frowned, then got to his feet hesitantly. The returning dizziness blotted out all doubt that the others were right. He reached for the new shirt, drew it on slowly. Hardin's eyes kept flicking fearfully through the door.

Janet returned with slickers and blankets. While Crockett and Hardin slipped into the slickers, she went back inside the store and soon returned with a package of food she'd made up. After Hardin took the package, she stood with her strained, pale face shadowed beneath the overhanging light, watching, holding her hands locked together in front of her.

"We'll be back in the morning," Crockett said to Allison.

"Not me," Hardin said. "I'm leavin' t'night. I won't be back."

"I'll be back," Crockett said quietly. His eyes met Janet's, caught her gentle stare watching him closely. He felt a sudden need to say something to make up for the way he'd snapped at her.

"Come on!" Hardin pleaded. "Before the rain lets up!"

Crockett's eyes stayed on the girl for another moment, then shifted to Allison. "Thanks . . . thanks," he said, and followed Fred Hardin outside.

Chapter Fifteen

DURING the next hours Gould waited impatiently for Brazos. The evening faded into damp, cool darkness before Bol Taylor rode in alone from the flat northwest of Hobart.

Gould calmed a bit, waited until the marshal tied up and came onto the porch before he opened the door.

Once inside, Taylor halted. He blinked from the lamplight.

"You took long enough," Gould said. "Where is he?"

"Coming in like you wanted." Taylor stood stiffly, glanced at the shaded window. "But he wouldn't come in until the rain stopped. Said he wouldn't take a chance on his gun gettin' stuck in a wet holster."

"And you couldn't hurry him?"

"No one could've hurried him, Mr. Gould. You know how he gets. I had a hard enough time talking him into riding in alone. I told him it had to be played up as a grudge, with you out of it, but . . ."

"He's doing it my way, though?"

"Yes. But he's getting harder to handle all the time. I think . . ."

"It'll be all right then," Gould said. "When he finishes this, I'll worry about handling him." He spoke quietly, aware of the importance of his statement. Today's events had proved it. Because Brazos was too quick to kill, this whole trouble had started. Because Brazos would kill, and that killing was legal by frontier standards, he was still necessary. But there was a limit to any man's use.

Taylor took a step toward the door. "I should make a round before he shows. I can fix it so I'm close to Allison's."

"No. You be at the other end of town. When it's over I want the mob to get there before you do. And keep your eyes on Cox. I don't want any eager kid deputy spoiling this.''

The marshal nodded, turned, left the office. Gould doused the lamp and raised the shade high so he could follow everything along the street and walks.

He scowled as he thought of Brazos Helm. Actually, his first mistake had been in listening to people back in Austin. He'd need a gunhand, they'd said, one the Texans would fear, and they'd gotten him Brazos. Gould had felt the danger of having a killer along right from the start, but they'd demanded it in Austin. They depended on fear as much as money or power. And the campaign built on fear had worked, up to the day they'd struck a rancher who wouldn't be frightened. . . .

Now Gould straightened, then leaned back from the window as he caught sight of the horse and rider emerging from the shadowed alleyway beyond the blacksmith's shop.

He watched Brazos Helm ride slowly to the hitchrail in front of the hotel and dismount.

Brazos hesitated a moment and with a deft, quick gesture hitched up his gun rig so it hung just right. Then he stepped onto the walk to cross the hotel porch.

Gould's gaze did not follow Brazos directly. For a fraction of a second it rested on the two-story hotel, the building's newness standing out clearly against the drab, weatherbeaten shacks and adobes beyond it. He had built that, and this building, too. These, the mansion he was putting up, the cattle empire he was developing—no one would tear them down now.

Not with the threat the Crocketts had held over him gone.

Gould was smiling as his gaze shifted to Brazos, just going up the steps of Allison's General Store.

Six of the town men had stopped in Allison's to find out how young Ben was doing, and gradually the masculine talk had drifted to the happenings of the day. They stood or sat around the cracker barrel halfway down the center aisle, near the dry goods counter. Pitkin Allison had joined them, leaving Janet working alone to restock the shelves and counters lining the store's south wall.

"Ain't a question of right or wrong," said a bald old cowhand in his slow Texas drawl. "Fact is, Ruel Crockett fought 'gainst his own people. I say he deserved that beatin'."

"Mebe he did the first time," the man beside him said. "But I'm not sure 'bout this time. He saved Ben's life, no matter how you look at it."

"Well, you keep thinkin' that way." The old cowhand was determined. "I got no use fer bluebellies, never will have."

"Least he fought for what he believed, McCann," another man answered. "Enough of us hollered 'the Union be damned,' all durin' the war, but never did have the guts to fight for the Confederacy. And Ruel ain't no damn carpetbagger. He sent word for the rest of us to git maverickin' and make that drive to Abilene with him."

A low murmur broke out then, divided talk that split the group. Cowmen who'd found hope in the plan to make a trail drive felt a growing kinship for Crockett that hadn't found expression until now. Allison heard their remarks, was not surprised by the changing attitudes. But neither was he surprised that McCann and one or two of the others wouldn't change. They'd lost sons or brothers in the war, and their pent-up hatred wouldn't die for a long time, maybe never.

"I'm not so sure I'm not glad Texas is still in the Union," he said. Waiting to judge the reaction to his remark, he saw that something in the rush of damp wind coming into the room had stilled the others, making them suddenly tense.

That was what warned Allison, that and the sound of the front door closing quietly. The storekeeper glanced around, following the men's stares, and saw Brazos Helm.

Brazos had halted just inside the door and stood surveying the men. He half-smiled casually, letting his gaze wander past each face and beyond to the door of the back room. His eyes narrowed and he glared as he started forward, hand poised above his six-gun.

He stalked to a spot three feet from Allison, his eyes missing nothing, then stopped with his back to the south wall, like a rattlesnake always ready to strike. He'd

noted Janet's position at the back counter and saw how
the men cleared the aisle to make a way if he wanted to
pass.

"There's talk Crockett's lookin' for me," he said in a
loud voice. "You tell him I'm here." He watched the
back room as if he expected the door to open.

"Ruel's not here," Allison said.

"I was told you brung him here after he got that
spankin' today."

"I did, but he's gone now."

"Then maybe I oughtta give you a little somethin',
huh?" Brazos still spoke loudly, his voice fast and
nasty now that he saw his crude attempts to draw
Crockett out were failing.

He started ahead again. Allison, his wrinkled face
tight, did not know what to expect. The others shrank
back close to the counter, clearing an even wider path.
Brazos Helm's half-smile was frozen onto his face.

When he reached the door, he exploded into motion.
He turned the knob and kicked the door open, drawing
the Starr in the same motion, then he barged into the
room. The whole thing was done with incredible speed,
the movements perfectly executed.

Brazos saw the room was empty and reappeared in
the doorway in a split second. He glanced around wildly,
then walked stiff-legged and angrily back to where Allison stood.

"Where'd he go?"

"I don't know. He left after he got strong enough."

Nodding, the gunman slid the Starr back into its holster. His face was calm, the picture of patience. "You
tell Crockett it was me who got Johnny," he said. "Tell
him I turned his hat over to Gould. You tell him that."

Allison flushed. He said, "In the back. You shot him
in the back."

Brazos nodded again. "Tell him I got the two thousand," he said, his voice quietly goading the old storekeeper. "Two thousand, you tell him."

Red-faced, Allison glared. The drawn breaths of the
watching men were loud in the silence. Only Allison
looked Brazos in the eye, the others glancing away from
his steady gaze, studying the floor, walls and piles of

goods and clothing on the counters. Janet stood staring, her hands clasped together near her throat.

"My boy," Allison said quietly. "You left my boy out there to be killed, too."

"That was a mistake," Brazos said bluntly. "Didn't figure Crockett'd be that bad a shot."

Allison, his face suddenly white with desperation, flung himself at Brazos. A slight raising of Brazos' arm held the old man off. The other arm came around in a backhand that staggered him, knocked him sprawling backwards. Allison careened off the shoe counter and crumpled to the floor beneath the gun rack, gasping for breath.

Brazos' glance checked the others, his eyes returning to Allison with a flicker. And he saw that the old storekeeper was pulling himself up, one hand reaching towards the racked guns.

"Go 'head," Brazos said. He chuckled, waited, his wolf-gray eyes shining in anticipation.

"Don't, Pit," a man called. "Don't!"

"He's an old man, Brazos," another said. Then, looking into the savage face, cried, "No! . . . He's an old man!"

Allison's hand dropped, and he just sat there, his bony face reddened where he'd taken the blow. For a long minute Brazos stared thoughtfully at the storekeeper.

His glance returned to the men, raking their faces, and they recoiled. He spoke to Allison.

"That's nothin' to what you can get, amigo. You tell Crockett I'm waitin'. I can come back, amigo."

Then, backing slowly to the door, he left the store.

Fred Hardin was worried and afraid. Usually by this time of night he had hours of drinking behind him, but now he was stone-sober. Since Ruel Crockett had fallen into an exhausted sleep late this afternoon, Hardin had kept watch, aware of every sound that came—animals moving about in the thicket and timber near the buildings, men, horses, vehicles on the road, night sounds drifting down from Hobart. He'd paced the length of the barn a hundred times, his stiff-legged limp shuffling in an uneven pattern. He hadn't bothered to light the lantern they'd brought along. He knew every inch of the dirt floor, and the darkness gave him a feeling of security that helped ease his fear.

He wasn't certain what he'd do once Crockett woke. He wasn't certain of anything except that he had to run. The thought of running, the sureness of it, kept repeating itself in his mind.

He paused in the deep darkness inside the doorway to peer out at the road and the town beyond. The sky was clearing, and the brightness of the moon streaked down in a dozen thick slices through wide breaks in the clouds, reflecting silver on the wet rooftops. Hardin knew that within another hour the prairie would be brilliantly lit, giving him less chance to get away. He shivered suddenly, partly at the thought, mainly at the new sound he picked up from the road.

It was a footstep squelching in the mud. A second came, then another, this time closer to the barn. Hardin turned fast and ran back to the last stall. Crouching down, he grabbed Crockett's shoulder and shook him.

Crockett woke immediately. "What . . . Fred?"

"Don't talk," Hardin whispered. "Someone's coming." His hand touched Crockett's side, feeling for the holstered Colt. "I'll . . ."

In one quick motion Crockett was up, with the .44 in his hand. He felt rested. Though a little unsteady on his feet, the heavy painful throbbing had gone from his head and body. He held onto the side of the stall. "Stay back, Fred . . . back," he said.

The moonlight outlined the large arch of the barn doorway. From beyond, the approaching footsteps made a loud sucking noise in the mud, splashing water. He waited, feeling the cool dampness of the night wind blowing on his face. He was wide awake now, stronger, prepared.

"Ruel?" The single word spoken near the door was just above a whisper, but it cut like a snake's rattle through the tense quiet. "Ruel, are you in there?" Then, the small figure of a woman appeared in the wide doorway, silhouetted against the moonlight.

"In here, Janet," Crockett said.

Janet Bankhead ran down the length of the barn.

When she could see Crockett, she broke into speech, "Ruel, Brazos is looking for you. You've . . ."

"Quiet," Crockett ordered, his voice low and hard. "You might've been followed." He took her arm, pulled her into the shadows.

Instant silence fell, and they stood motionless, listening. During the next few minutes nothing broke the stillness of the night except the shifting of one of the horses in the opposite stalls.

Finally Crockett said, "Brazos is in town?"

"Yes," she answered, then told him quickly what had happened in Allison's store. "He's waiting for you. He'll jump you as soon as you show up." She drew a long breath, and he felt a little shiver run through her body and the arm he was holding.

Crockett said bitterly, "After murdering Johnny, he'll back up that threat to Allison unless I go in."

"But Mr. Allison said for you to stay here. He'll keep out of Brazos' way."

"No, he'll be in danger until this is over." He realized he was still holding her arm, yet he did not want to let go. "I'll speak to Bol Taylor before . . ."

"Don't do that!" Fred Hardin said suddenly. "You can't go to Bol Taylor. He won't do you no good."

Looking at the old man, Crockett said, "Bol's marshal, Fred. Brazos won't go through a lawman."

Hardin shook his head quickly. "If Brazos wants to go after Allison, Bol won't stop him. Not if Gould says . . ." He stopped talking.

There was a heavy silence. Shortly, Crockett asked, "What about Gould, Fred?" He let Janet's arm go.

Even in the dim light filtering through the half-completed roof, Crockett could see Hardin's sheepish look, how the old man glanced uncomfortably at his boots while he cleared his throat nervously.

"What are you afraid of, Fred?"

Hardin shifted his feet uneasily. He stared first at Janet and then at Crockett, as if he didn't know what to do next.

"I'm going into town, Fred," said Crockett in a solemn voice. "I'll keep under cover until I make sure Allison's safe with Bol Taylor. After that I'll see how far Brazos wants to go.'' He turned towards the barn.

Fred Hardin said quickly, ''Ruel, I'm leavin'.'' He hesitated, swallowing against something hard in his throat. ''You won't try to stop me, Ruel?''

''Any reason why I should, Fred?''

Hardin's body was stiff in the agony of indecision. ''You gotta understand how it was, Ruel!'' he pleaded. ''They had Jason beat me. They wouldn't let me 'lone for a minute. And Brazos was always close. You gotta understand!''

Crockett stared at the white-haired old man, seeing the same desperate fear riding Hardin that he'd seen that first time inside the barn. He nodded slowly, watching Hardin.

''What is it, Fred?''

Hardin looked down at the ground. ''They came out to see your Paw,'' he said, his voice uneven, trembling. ''Gould brought Howells along with the money for the ranch. Brazos and Jason were there, too. Bol Taylor was county deputy then. I guess he was along 'cause they figgered he was the law.''

In the dark Hardin could feel the others stiffen. He glanced up now, and his words came slower. ''Your Paw, he'd been down with the flu, but he got up and told them they'd better git 'cause he wasn't sellin'. When they wouldn't go, he came to the door with his Old Betsy. Brazos drew on him, shot him right where he stood.''

''You saw that?'' Crockett said in a soft, horrified voice. ''And you never told Johnny or me?''

The old man took an involuntary step backward, as though he expected Crockett to come at him. ''I saw it,'' he breathed, choking on the words. ''There was nothing I could do. Brazos woulda turned his gun on me if Howells hadn't stopped him.''

He hesitated, his rough old fists tightening. ''They made me bury him,'' he said softly. ''Then Jason and Brazos stayed out at the ranch with me two whole months. They kept me long enough so's I couldn't talk without bein' blamed, too. That Jason beat me once, beat me so's I couldn't walk two days, just 'cause I tried to get down to the spring. And Brazos was always around with his gun, Ruel. I...''

"Johnny had been back a good three months, Fred."

"I didn't dare tell him. They'd've gunned him, too. Then, when he talked 'bout selling Diamond C . . . I don't know, Ruel. I couldn't tell Johnny. Not with Jason there. Not with Brazos' gun ready all the time."

"It was easier to swill whisky." Crockett said, fury burning his sore, bruised face like a white-hot iron. "Easier to keep drunk all the time— Was that it?"

Hardin's shoulders slumped, and he refused to meet Crockett's hard eyes.

Crockett watched him a while, then took a step toward the stalls that held the horses. "All right, run, Fred," he said. "I won't hold you."

The old man simply stared at him, his expression indistinguishable in the blackness. Janet Bankhead moved alongside Crockett, grabbed his sleeve and held him back. "Ruel, what are you going to do?" she said.

"I'm going to face Brazos."

"No. You're in no shape to—"

"It's time now," he said. The shock of his father's being so brutally killed had dulled some, and now he also thought of Johnny's twisted, still body lying where Brazos had left him behind Allison's store. He continued.

Janet kept after him. "Let the law—"

"Bol Taylor's the law." He snapped a glance back at Hardin. "You ride out first, Fred. I'll give you time." He began pulling his saddle down from the top of the stall.

"No," Janet said pleadingly. "You're doing this wrong. Even if you beat Brazos, you won't be touching the men behind him. But if Fred stays you can bring them all into the open. You'll have a witness who'll stand up in any court."

Crockett stopped short, realizing that she was right. Making Brazos pay wasn't enough. Janet's way would get those who turned the mad dog loose. He stared at Hardin.

"If you're willing to stay, we can get them all, Fred."

"No . . . no," said Hardin. "I gotta run. Brazos . . ."

"I'll handle Brazos," Crockett said calmly.

"I can't," Hardin whimpered, gesturing toward the

night. "I have a chance if I ride now. If I wait 'til mornin', I . . ."

"Fred," said Crockett, "give me an hour. I'll come back once I take care of Brazos." He saw Hardin flinch in understanding and added, "If I don't come back in an hour, Fred, you'll still have time to ride away from here."

"I don't . . ." Hardin swallowed hard, and then his voice steadied grimly. "An hour, Ruel. You aren't back, I'm goin'."

Crockett nodded. He drew the Henry carbine from its boot and rested it against the stall. He bent to lift the saddle again, but the touch of Fred Hardin's hand on his arm made him look up.

Hardin said, "You understand, Ruel? You understand why I couldn't tell?" He breathed deeply and rubbed a hand over his wrinkled face. "You understand?"

"I understand, Fred," Crockett told him quietly.

But Hardin wasn't content to let it go at that. "It was Brazos and Jason. That beatin' . . ." He rubbed his face anxiously. "Your Paw kept me on after I hurt my leg, Ruel. I . . . I could only forget things if I was drunk, Ruel."

Again Crockett nodded. He did not want to watch Hardin go on like this, feeling that he should leave the man alone with his terrible burden of guilt. He bent again and lifted the saddle.

When he straightened, Janet said, "Don't try to out-draw Brazos. He's . . ."

"I'm not out to beat him in a gunfight," Crockett said, heaving the saddle up over the top of the stall. "I want Brazos at that trial, too. And he'll be there."

He glanced at her, saw her concerned stare. He put one hand gently on her slim shoulder.

"They could be waiting outside town," he said. "You wait here with Fred. I'll come back for you, too."

She looked around toward where the old man stood alone and dejected. "I'll wait, Ruel," she said.

Crockett's hand dropped from her shoulder. Without speaking, he picked up the Henry, slid it under his arm and walked out of the barn.

Chapter Sixteen

NOT MANY PEOPLE were outside tonight. Word had spread that Brazos was out hunting, and people here knew too well that in these gunfights innocent bystanders were often hit by wild bullets. When one of the more reckless pedestrians did come along the walk, Taylor, who had hidden himself near Allison's, ducked back into the deep shadows of the alleyway, making sure he couldn't be seen.

He kept watching the porch of the hotel where Brazos Helm stood waiting directly beneath a bright lamp. Taylor wasn't certain that Crockett would show, but he was sure Gould wouldn't let up until both Crockett and Fred Hardin were dead. Things were too close now to have it any other way.

Taylor felt faintly sorry for Crockett. He was, after all, the victim of Brazos Helm's stupid blunder in killing old Ted Crockett. Gould hadn't wanted it that way, but after it happened they were all in too deep to let the story get out.

Now, shifting uncomfortably from the long wait, Taylor reached into a back pocket for his plug of tobacco. He bit in, began chewing, then spat out everything when he saw Al Cox coming hurriedly along the walk.

The tall deputy started cutting across Pioneer toward the jail. Taylor waited until he drew closer.

"Al," he called in a loud voice.

Cox whirled on his heel, his hand dropping as if he expected to have to use his guns. He stopped the drop when he saw Taylor.

"Where are you going, Al?" Taylor beckoned to the young deputy, then stepped back deeper into the shadows.

With a quick glance back along the street, Cox came in toward the walk. "Crockett's comin'," he said.

"That's no concern of yours, Al," said Taylor.

"Brazos shot Johnny Crockett in the back. I'm gonna get my shotgun."

Taylor's hand fell, came up with his Colt. "They'll settle it their own way, Al. You step in here." His voice became gruff, impatient. "Now, Al."

Cox frowned, then stepped across the walk into the alleyway.

Brazos Helm had purposely picked the brilliantly lighted hotel porch as his place to wait. For one reason, Crockett would be at a disadvantage having to come at him facing the glare of the lamplight. For another, Brazos wanted to be where everyone would see him doing his job. He was aware of Bol Taylor and Cox over there in the alleyway, just as he was aware of all the people watching him from the saloons, windows, and doorways. This was an old, familiar pattern for Brazos, and he enjoyed it. Unhurried, calm, he gave a hitch to his belt, edging the heavy Starr .44 slightly higher as his gaze raked the length of Pioneer.

If he figured right, Cox's hurrying from the back of town meant Crockett was going to make his play. That's what he expected now, what he was planning on.

One second later he knew he was right, for he saw Crockett turn out of the alleyway beyond the general store. A smile cracked Brazos' lips.

Crockett halted in the shadows of the porch to study Pioneer Street.

Contemptuously, Brazos reached into his shirt pocket for his tobacco. He played to his audience, rolling a cigarette with his left hand. He indicated no awareness of Crockett, merely waited, feet planted firmly on the flooring of the porch.

In the silence of the street a man swore softly. Brazos caught that, felt satisfaction run through him. But within he was not careless, nor casual. He waited, ready to drop the half-rolled cigarette and act fast. Playing to the crowd was one thing, but he'd lived by the gun too long to ever chance underestimating an enemy.

Crockett was moving again, stepping out into the center of Pioneer. Brazos saw the rifle cradled in the tall man's arm.

Suddenly, the withdrawn crowd no longer mattered to Brazos. His six-gun was no match for the Henry at this distance. Cursing himself for bragging about killing Crockett's brother, he slid the cigarette between his lips. He didn't light it; he just stood and waited.

Ruel Crockett took careful, slow steps. The walk back into Hobart hadn't been long, but it had tired him. Each time he lifted a boot the mud seemed to suck it back. The rifle was a dead weight in his arms.

He studied the doorways and windows carefully. The whole town was up for this one, even the women and kids. He kept going ahead, alert, the blood pulsing coldly through his veins.

When he knew he'd almost reached the range of Brazos' gun, he raised the Henry and pointed it directly at the gunman's chest.

"Helm," he called. "I'm taking you in for killing my father. Come down here."

Brazos stiffened. "Your father? I heard you wanted to see me 'bout Johnny . . . and Ben Allison."

"Later," Crockett said calmly. "This comes first. Now, come down—careful."

"You ain't no lawman, Crockett. Come and get me."

Anger coursed through Brazos, anger tinged with disappointment. There would be no preliminaries to a shootout. He would feel none of the intense joy of staring a man down while he waited for the draw, none of the exultation that came after the kill, no enjoyment of the crowd's reaction. He saw the muzzle of the Henry lower an inch to the pit of his stomach, and then he heard Crockett's words.

"One second, Brazos. Try anything and you'll die slow."

"Brave man," Brazos sneered and walked carefully down the porch steps toward Crockett, keeping his eyes on Crockett's bruised face.

Suddenly Crockett was surrounded by the murmur of voices. The townspeople had left their hiding places and were converging on the two, forming a wide circle around them. He spoke loudly so the watchers could hear. "Who was with you when you killed my father, Brazos?"

"I don't know nothin' 'bout your father." Brazos

stopped two feet away from Crockett. "You got no right doin' this. You want to face me, put that rifle down and do it like a man."

"Gould was with you, wasn't he? Howells and Jason, too. And Bol . . ."

A wild shout came from the rear of the crowd. "Fight Brazos or back out, you damyankee bluebelly! I'll handle the law here!"

Crockett knew Bol Taylor's voice, but he had to risk a glance. The marshal was still beyond the crowd and he could not see him. Then, more shouting came: "Crockett! Watch it, Crockett! Brazos!"

Brazos was on him before Crockett could use the Henry. Brazos pushed the rifle barrel aside, grabbed at it with his left hand while the right streaked for his own revolver. The sudden act tore the Henry from Crockett's weakened hands. Still keeping his head, Crockett lunged forward, using the weight of his body to knock Brazos off balance.

Brazos staggered, but, using the fast triggering of the professional gunman, he got off his first shot. The bullet zinged past Crockett's ear and continued on over the heads of the people. The screaming crowd spread out like a huge fan in its dash for cover.

Brazos' second bullet tore through Crockett's shirt, grazing the skin along his ribs. But there was no third shot. Crockett, crouching to make a smaller target while he drew, shot once, then again. Blood gushed from Brazos' neck.

The gunman straightened, a look of amazed shock crossing his face. Still clutching his revolver, he rocked unsteadily, straining to shoot again.

Crockett held his fire as he saw Brazos' fingers loosen on the Starr's handle. As the Starr dropped like a heavy weight and Brazos' knees buckled, Crockett whipped around toward the crowd, moving to the left as he searched for Bol Taylor.

But he saw no sign of the marshal. The townspeople were closing in again, silent this time, staring down at the man who had terrorized them for so long. One or two shouts sounded now, but most of the onlookers just moved forward quietly, gasping, staring in disbelief.

Crockett dropped to his knees beside Brazos. One of his bullets had smashed through the gunman's right shoulder; the other had ripped along the neck just two inches above the first wound. From Brazos' grunting breath he knew the killer was dying. The unlit cigarette still clung to the dry lips.

"Brazos," he said, "who was with you when you killed my father?"

Brazos' eyes rolled, focused on Crockett. "Y— you . . ."

"Who was with you?" Crockett shouted.

"Go t' . . . go . . ."

Crockett leaned closer to Brazos. "Was Gould there? Did he order you to shoot?"

A hand touched Crockett's shoulder. Pitkin Allison said, "He's dead, Ruel."

For a moment Crockett knelt there in the mud, oblivious of the water seeping around his legs, staring into the dead man's face. Suddenly he pushed himself up, tearing free of Allison's grip.

Crockett shoved against the men who were crowded in close and began breaking his way through the rest of the crowd.

Behind him Pitkin Allison picked up Crockett's Henry. "Ruel," he called. "Your rifle, Ruel!"

But Crockett didn't hear. He was already halfway out of the crowd, headed for Gould's land and stock building. Allison's words were drowned out by the thunderous murmuring of the crowd.

Bol Taylor had gotten almost through the crowd when Brazos fell. Right then Taylor had ducked back, turned and started to run away.

Franklin Gould, watching from the doorway of his office, knew what had happened immediately when he saw the marshal break out of the crowd and head his way.

The stockman's smooth forehead wrinkled in puzzled disbelief, but his thoughts didn't linger on Brazos. He'd have to plan fast, to make a shift in his actions. The death of a gunman was simply a tally on the balance sheet, a business expenditure he'd eventually have to afford someday anyway. It didn't matter too much now.

Scrip for land was what had brought him here, and he had all he needed. He could be thousands of miles away and still get all the benefits of ownership.

Calmly, Gould waited until Taylor reached the porch steps.

"Crockett killed Brazos," Taylor called. "He knows about Ted being shot. We gotta run . . ."

"All right, Bol," Gould said, staring beyond the marshal to the crowd, which had closed in around the scene of battle like a milling herd of cattle. "You'll need a horse, Bol. I'll tell Howells. We'll meet you out at my house."

The mustached lawman turned and started along the porch. Gould, still watching the crowd, saw that those lining the rear were opening a way, and he knew Crockett was coming. He needed time now, and Taylor could give him that.

"Bol, take a horse from there," he called, motioning toward the animals racked in front of the saloon in the adjoining block.

He waited long enough to make certain Taylor followed the advice. Then he retreated inside the office.

Taylor made a run for the horses. He reached the closest, a big black stallion, just as he noticed Crockett crossing Pioneer toward him. He made no attempt to untie the animal. Crouching, he dashed for the closest alleyway. He'd gotten only ten feet into the deep shadows between the buildings before Crockett's voice cracked behind him.

"Stop right there, Bol."

The marshal whirled around like a clumsy mule. He stared at Crockett openmouthed, his face frozen. "I didn't kill your Pa, Ruel," he offered. "I was just there. I didn't have nothin' to do with it."

"Come out here, Bol. . . . Slow now!"

Taylor lifted his hands high, so Crockett could see they were well clear of his gunbelt. His voice rose higher. "I don't want to fight you, Ruel."

Moving to the end of the alleyway, close to Taylor, Crockett jerked the lawman's Colt from its holster.

"Where's Gould?" Above his own words Crockett heard running footsteps behind him. Turning, he saw it was Pitkin Allison. The elderly storekeeper carried his Henry rifle.

"Gould's inside," Taylor said. "He was just on the porch."

Allison was beside Crockett now. "You fergot this," he panted, holding out the Henry.

Crockett took the rifle. "You take Taylor over to the jail," he said. He gave Allison Taylor's revolver. "Tell Cox I'll make charges later."

Seeing Allison's nod, Crockett headed for the front door of Gould's office.

For a moment Taylor gazed after Crockett. "Pit, let me go," he said. "I didn't kill Ted Crockett."

"Ruel says you were there, Bol."

"They'll hang me, Pit." The mustached lawman could see that others in the street had noticed what was going on and that some of them were starting toward him. Fearfully, he took a step closer to Allison. "I'm not going to hang, Pit. You hear me?"

"Get back, Bol. I don't want to shoot you, but . . ."

"Let me go! I've got to go!" Taylor's voice was shrill, almost a shriek as he swung out, hitting the old storekeeper on the jaw.

Allison fell back and lay there, stunned. Taylor pounced on him, caught in the frenzy of his fear, hammering both fists into the small wrinkled face. When he straightened again, he held his own Colt, and Allison was a limp unconscious form.

Taylor took one last terrified glance toward the street. "They won't hang me . . . won't hang me," he whimpered, then ran into the blackness of the alleyway.

Chapter Seventeen

CROCKETT kicked open the door to Gould's office, let it slam back before he charged in. The room was empty and papers were scattered on the desk, a few on the floor. Every drawer was open, the contents disarranged as if Gould had rumpled through them quickly, grabbing only certain items. Crockett started around the desk, but he halted abruptly when he saw Johnny's sombrero in the double bottom drawer.

Momentarily, he hesitated and stared down at the sombrero, feeling a pang of sorrow blend with his anger. The room was still and quiet. He knew that everything was just about over for the men who'd killed his father and brother, but an impatient restlessness burned in him to end it completely. His heavy bitterness built up a pressure within him that took away all tiredness, giving him power and drive.

He went on, through the back room and out into the darkness. He moved slowly, carefully, for he wasn't sure that he wasn't stepping right into the sights of a gun in Gould's hands. He had no illusions about himself. He'd been the one Gould had worried about all along, and if he was killed the stockman could handle Fred Hardin easily.

His eyes accustomed to the darkness now, he made out a set of footprints in the mud, new prints which were not yet completely filled with water. He eased along the wall, breathing hard as he made a dash across the open alleyway to the next building.

Gould had circled around behind the line of stores and saloons fronting on Pioneer, heading for the hotel. Now that he was sure where his prey had gone, Crockett speeded his pace.

The alleyway beside the hotel was empty. He broke into a run, still keeping close to the building so the bright moonlight and yellow lamplight streaming down into the puddles near the porch wouldn't cast a telltale shadow.

He went up onto the porch and into the lobby. The clerk, a stubby, balding man with a Robert E. Lee beard, stared wide-eyed at the Henry rifle.

"Franklin Gould?" was all Crockett said.

"In his room," the clerk answered. "Top of the stairs." He gestured wildly, his fear ample proof he hadn't lied.

Crockett went up the stairs, keeping his head low, moving as quietly as possible.

The door to Gould's room was wide open. Crockett charged in, holding the Henry out, ready for instant fire. The room was empty, drawers open. Hastily pulled-out clothing was lying on the floor or hanging down from the dresser.

Swinging around, Crockett went out into the hallway and along the pine floor to Howells' rooms. He stopped at the door. Low, quick conversation sounded inside.

Crockett raised his right foot, kept the Henry waist high as he kicked hard, then moved into the room through the smashed-open door.

Marion and William Howells, standing in the middle of the parlor, whirled to face him. The look of amazed shock was wiped from the woman's lovely face almost instantly, but she stared dumbfoundedly into Crockett's swollen bruised face. Her brother watched Crockett, terrified. trying to catch his breath.

"Where's Gould?" Crockett asked William Howells.

"He's gone. He was here but . . ." Marion stopped talking when she saw Crockett shifting the rifle's muzzle to her brother, who was edging back toward his bedroom. "No!" she said. "No, don't shoot!"

"Back here," Crockett said to Howells.

Holding himself rigid, Howells took short steps back to the center of the room. Crockett couldn't see the sling on his arm because of the coat he was wearing, but the banker kept his left side stiff, favoring it.

"William hasn't done anything," Marion said, her voice low. "Franklin Gould was here, and he told him to get out of town. But William hasn't done anything wrong." She was nervous, passionately sincere.

Crockett said to Howells, "You figure you could get far with that arm?"

Howells swallowed. "I didn't know. I tried . . ."

"I wouldn't let him go," Marion said. "If Gould has done something wrong, William had no part in it."

For a moment Crockett stared at her, watching the expression on her face. He was convinced she knew nothing of what had happened.

"You tell her," he said to Howells.

Howells turned a sickly white. He wouldn't look at his sister. "I had nothing to do with it," he sputtered, motioning with his good arm. "I didn't know it would happen."

"You were there."

"Yes," Howells answered wearily. "And I've been living with it ever since. But you wouldn't believe that."

Marion gazed from one man to the other, her eyebrow lifted, questioning her brother. "William," she said, "tell me?"

All color drained from around the banker's thin mouth as he bit down on his lips.

She said, "Did you know they'd killed Johnny like that, William? Did you have him killed?"

"No!" Howells said. "It was Crockett's father . . . before you got here. We went out to their ranch. It was supposed to be a quick sale, but he wouldn't sell." He hesitated, breathed the words. "Brazos killed him."

"And you were there?" she said weakly.

Howells nodded and shut his eyes, as if trying to blot out any remembrance of the shooting. "I couldn't stop him, he shot so fast. After it was done I could only do what Gould said."

"A man was murdered, William." Marion spoke quietly, as if to a little child. Watching her, Crockett saw the way the skin had tightened along her fine cheeks, how she was completely without motion except for her moving lips.

"I couldn't do anything," Howells said, shaking his head, looking at her hopelessly. "Gould would've dragged me in on it." Suddenly he flinched. "Crockett's hired hand saw it. They beat him so he'd keep quiet. They would've beaten me. You were coming here. I couldn't run. I couldn't do anything but stay."

"And you won't run now," Marion ordered. "You won't meet Gould."

"Meet Gould?" Crockett cut in. "When?"

"Now," she said. "Gould told William to get what he could from the bank and meet him at his house. We were to leave from there."

Crockett's face tightened, the fear in his mind stiffening his whole body. Gould would stumble on Janet Bankhead and Fred Hardin. He swung around on his heel and started for the door.

"Don't go out there alone," Marion said. "We're both supposed to meet Gould. William sent Anna for our buggy. If I go with you, Gould will think it's William and me."

"It's dangerous for you," Crockett said. "I don't know."

She came close to him and put her hand on his. "You'll have a chance that way. Please . . . ," she said. She glanced at the door as a noise came from the hallway.

The small Mexican servant came through the doorway. When she saw Crockett holding the Henry she stopped short, glancing indecisively from Marion to the rifle.

"Is the buggy ready, Anna?" Marion asked.

The dark-skinned girl nodded. "*Sí*. Out back, señorita."

"You stay with Mr. Howells," Marion told the servant. She paused and looked at her brother. "You'll wait here, William?"

Howells stared at her like a man in a daze. He fell back into the overstuffed chair. "I'll wait," he said, his voice low, hoarse with strain.

She nodded and started for the hallway. Crockett went out behind her.

Chapter Eighteen

THE BUGGY was waiting behind the hotel. When the Mexican handy-man, who was holding the team of matched bays saw Marion and Crockett coming, he let go the lines and got down to the ground.

Marion thanked him, but she didn't climb up. She stopped at the step plate and stood there, her hand touching her cheek as she looked at Crockett.

"What's the matter?" he asked.

"Maybe I should drive," she said. "Gould will be

expecting William and me. And he knows William can't drive with a bad shoulder. If a man's driving, he might suspect something."

Crockett nodded, pleased with her quick thinking. "Just go as fast as you would if your brother was here. You'll do all right."

He held her arm while she mounted, then walked around behind the vehicle and climbed into the leather seat beside her. He slouched a little, sitting as though favoring his right side. The Henry lay ready across his lap.

Crockett was worried about Janet and Fred Hardin, but he hoped that their being in the barn behind the house had allowed them time to hear Gould coming. He held onto that hope.

"Ruel," Marion said, "I didn't know anything about it."

"I know. I didn't suspect anything either. I got a letter from my father a month before. He'd had a cold all winter. I didn't question pneumonia."

"Besides William and Gould, who was there?" Her face was grim.

"Jason, Brazos and Bol Taylor. I think your brother was telling the truth. It should've only been a business trip, but Brazos spoiled that."

"Brazos," she said, a note of weariness in her tone. "William had no reason to be working with a man like him. No reason at all."

"Gould's kind will use anyone, Marion."

"William could only do as he was told," she said. "He must have been as ashamed as he was frightened. If it was only fright he would've told me. He's always been so weak."

Crockett watched her sympathetically. In the brightness of the moonlight her face was a tense mask. The damp creek wind fluttered her skirt and stirred her hair, and, except for the slight movements of her hands, she was completely still.

"I'm sorry about your father and Johnny," she said, not taking her eyes from the horses. "I'm truly sorry. But my brother ..."

His hand on her arm silenced her. A shadowy movement ahead had materialized into the figure of a man coming their way. Even as the team slowed, he knew it was Fred Hardin from the bent-over posture and listing gait. Crockett breathed deeply, experiencing sudden relief.

"Fred..."

Hardin limped quickly to the buggy. His glance slid from Crockett to the woman beside him.

Crockett said, "Where's Janet, Fred?"

"Hid back in the oaks." He was breathing rapidly, his wrinkled face tense with excitement. "She's good n' safe. Gould's at the house, Ruel. Him and Bol Taylor."

At mention of the marshal, Crockett felt a quiver of concern for Pitkin Allison go down his spine, his fear of what had happened to the old storekeeper blending with his thoughts of what lay ahead. It wasn't over yet; it could all fall through right here, with two of them to take.

"You get back to Janet, Fred," he said.

Fred Hardin reached up and grabbed Crockett's arm. "They're scared, Ruel. I heard them talkin'. They're scared and they're runnin'. I'll go back with you."

Crockett hesitated. Gould was the man who'd terrorized Hardin, who'd weakened him. Now, Hardin saw fear in Gould and understood the full extent of the stockman's weakness. It was a bold move, but the old cowhand wasn't ready for it.

"No, Fred," he said. "If they're scared, they'll be all the more dangerous."

Hardin shook his head. "They beat me, Ruel. They made me so's I couldn't look you in the face. Don't you see, Ruel?"

"Fred, you take care of Janet," said Crockett. He held out the Henry. "If anything goes wrong, you see they don't touch her."

When Hardin took the rifle, Marion started the buggy forward again. For the first few feet Hardin tried to follow, but when the horses increased their pace, the old man fell behind.

They rode in silence. After another half-minute Crockett could see the lighter line of the drive cutting through the timber to the wide yard. The buildings ahead were bulky black shapes beyond the edge of the moonlit clearing.

"Slow now," he told Marion.

"Ruel," she said. "What will happen to William?"

"I don't know."

"He's afraid, too, Ruel," she said, biting her lip. "He's weak, Ruel, but he's my brother. He came down here mainly for me. He thought he could make enough money to give us both a good life."

Crockett did not answer. He slouched over more, then drew his Colt and peered ahead, trying to separate the shadows of buildings and trees. The oaks beyond the house were dark and still, with no light filtering through. They could be waiting there. . . .

"You get out as soon as we stop," he said, wiping the cold sweat of his palms on his trousers. "I'll give you time to get away from the buggy before I begin shooting."

Marion seemed to shiver beside him, but her voice was calm as she spoke. "They'll hang William, won't they?"

"I don't know." He didn't want talk now, only quiet so he could listen. The mansion was clear, its shape black and ominous. He crouched even more. "Stop here," he said. "You'll stay here."

"No," she answered. "I'll go all the way." Somehow her voice had changed. The tone was harder now, and it made him glance at her. She sat straight, staring ahead uncertainly, her eyes searching the deep shadows.

"Too dangerous for you," he told her. "I'll go alone."

"No!" She shook the reins, studying him as she spoke, her mouth twisted and tense. "You were willing to lose Diamond C to save Johnny after he shot William."

"But there's no sense in your taking a chance on getting killed."

"I won't get killed," she said, drawing rein hard. Before the buggy was completely still, she stood up. Grabbing her skirt up in her hand, she began climbing over the side.

When her feet reached the muddy ground, Crockett

lifted the reins. "Walk back fast," he whispered. "I'll drive closer to the house."

"Ruel, I can't let them hang William." She stared up at him. Her face had lost its tense uncertainty, and now there was something violent in the way she watched him.

"Walk back," he said sharply. "Hurry while there's time."

"I can't let them hang him," she repeated. Then she turned and, as she began running toward the mansion, she yelled into the quiet darkness.

"It's Crockett, Franklin! Do you hear me, Franklin?" Crockett's in the bug—"

A sudden outbreak of gunfire cut her off in the middle of the word, three quick shots barking from the corner of the mansion. Marion's surprised, painful scream was loud and shrill, but it ceased instantly as she fell headlong into the mud.

Crockett's shock lasted only a fraction of a second. Then he crouched and faced in the direction of the gun flashes. He saw the figure of a man, a tall blur in the darkness. Crockett's gun sounded twice, and he heard Bol Taylor let out a high, incredulous cry of pain.

The horses' whinnys mixed with the echoes of the gunblasts, and the fear-crazed animals began running, jolting the buggy ahead.

Even as he'd triggered the shots Crockett had begun jumping to get clear of the open seat. But the sudden bolting of the animals knocked him off balance, and he had to grab at the side to keep his footing. He heard the blast of a second gun from the mansion's porch and saw the barrel flash as something slammed into his shoulder. The impact whipped him half-way around and sent him reeling back and down to the seat.

There was no pain at first. All feeling was gone. His brain was working furiously, screaming for him to get clear of the seat and behind cover. A second shot blasted away, and a slug shrieked past his head. He slid sideways and shoved his body up and over the side of the buggy, trying hard to fall clear of the turning wheels.

He struck the mud with a loud splash and skidded a few feet. Then, sprawled out, he tried to bring up the mud-covered Colt. His fingers had lost all their strength, and the gun slipped from his hand.

Wildly, he groped at the slimy mud, but he couldn't locate the Colt. He heard footsteps click along the mansion's veranda.

Crockett groveled on all fours like a trapped animal, digging in the mud with both hands. The white-hot pain hit him then, driving through his entire body with incredible speed, squeezing the breath from him. He stiffened and pressed both palms flat to keep from falling on his face.

Footsteps were heavy on the veranda steps, then loud on the muddy ground. Crockett raised his head and saw Gould coming toward him, his tall body blotting out the building behind him. The derringer he held looked as big as a buffalo gun.

"You stupid cowhand," Gould snarled, his eyes deadly. "You'd almost licked me, but your damned stubbornness wouldn't let you quit when you were ahead."

Crockett pushed himself up higher, fought the pain and sickness in his stomach. "You're all done," he said, the effort to talk bringing dizziness. "You're all done here."

"There are other places out in this country," Gould said. "I've got the scrip so—"

The sound of water splashing close by made him look back across the wide clearing. Lights were on in every building back in town, and from the distance came the faint confusion of excited shouting. Gould heard Fred Hardin's voice before he saw him.

"Gould . . . drop that gun, Gould!" The words were close, loud, with a sharpness to them.

Crockett turned his head, saw Hardin's bent-over form coming across the yard toward them. "Go back, Fred!" he yelled. "Go back!"

The old man didn't answer. He just kept coming ahead slowly, the Henry rifle he held raised to chest-level.

Before Crockett could call again, Gould shot Fred Hardin. The derringer's blast shattered the night, and the approaching form stopped short and began to fall.

"Now you," Gould said, lowering the stubby double

barrels down to Crockett's head. He leaned forward, speaking slowly and distinctly. "I've got your scrip and..."

Gould never heard the shot that sent a bullet ripping into his chest. He died instantly.

The blast of the gun kept pounding in Crockett's eardrums even after Gould fell. When he looked around, Fred Hardin was coming toward him again dragging his left side as though it was a dead weight.

"He got my game leg," Hardin said. He stopped beside Crockett and stared down at Gould's body. He leaned on the rifle, using it as a crutch.

"Got my game leg," he repeated in a low voice, then broke into sobbing quiet laughter, as though he'd made a joke that was somehow personally hilarious.

Crockett looked up at Hardin. "Thanks, Fred," he said. Then, he glanced back toward the spot where Marion had fallen. "See how she is, will you?"

Hardin nodded and moved slowly away. Crockett pushed hard with his right arm, twisting his body into a sitting position. During the next minute he remained quiet, controlling the intense pain and nausea his movement had brought on.

Fred Hardin called, "She's dead, Ruel."

Crockett didn't say anything. He stared at Marion's body until after Hardin had limped his way across the lawn to where Bol Taylor lay. Mercifully, the marshal's bullets had killed her instantly, so she hadn't suffered. He was glad at that, but felt nothing else for her but sorrow.

All the closeness he'd felt for her had been blown apart by her first yell to Gould.

The shouting from the road was loud now. He could see the first of the townspeople crowding up the drive to find out what the shooting had been about. One figure was way ahead of the rest, a woman, her skirt lifted as she ran stumbling through the mud.

"Ruel?" Janet Bankhead called. "Are you all right, Ruel?" Reaching Crockett, she knelt beside him.

"It's all over now," he told her quietly. He smiled faintly as he looked into her face and added, "Help me up, will you, Janet?"

She put her arm around his waist, moving closer so

he could hold her shoulder for support. As he pushed himself up, he could smell the sweet cleanliness of her hair close to his face.

"Slowly now," she said. "Do it slowly, Ruel."

Loud splashing sounded close behind them. "What happened here?" It was Al Cox. The young deputy's face was officious but cautious as he stared at the dead bodies.

"I'll tell you at Doc's," Crockett said. Though he was standing now, he hesitated, his eyes searching the mud for his Colt.

A sudden smile came over his face, and he straightened. "You'd better collect the guns around here so the town kids won't find them," he said to the deputy. Then, he put his arm around Janet's shoulder.

Janet stiffened at his weight, but she held on. Crockett was aware of the slight electric tingle that went through him at touching her. Vaguely, he remembered the bitterness he'd borne toward her, but that was all gone now. He held on tightly.

Al Cox said, "Here, I'll help you." He reached out to take Crockett's arm.

"I'm all right," said Crockett. And, seeing that Fred Hardin was coming toward them, said, "Help Fred. He got shot in the leg."

The deputy turned to Hardin. "You take my arm, Fred," he said.

"No," the old man answered. "You've got work to do. I'll make it okay." He gestured around the yard, pointing with a finger at the body near the mansion. "Bol Taylor's dead over there."

When he looked around again, he saw that Crockett and Janet had slowed a little to talk to Pitkin Allison, who'd come up with the townspeople.

For longer than a minute, Hardin stood quietly, watching. Then, standing straighter than he had in more than a year, he put his weight on his make-shift crutch and followed them from the yard.